An American Girl in Italy

AUBRIE DIONNE

A division of HarperCollins*Publishers*
www.harpercollins.co.uk

HarperImpulse an imprint of
HarperCollins*Publishers* Ltd
77–85 Fulham Palace Road
Hammersmith, London W6 8JB

www.harpercollins.co.uk

A Paperback Original 2014

First published in Great Britain in ebook format by HarperImpulse 2014

Copyright © Aubrie Dionne 2014

Cover images © Shutterstock.com

Aubrie Dionne asserts the moral right
to be identified as the author of this work

A catalogue record for this book is
available from the British Library

ISBN: 9780008104399

This novel is entirely a work of fiction.
The names, characters and incidents portrayed in it are
the work of the author's imagination. Any resemblance to
actual persons, living or dead, events or localities is
entirely coincidental.

Automatically produced by Atomik ePublisher from Easypress

For the Boston Youth Symphony Orchestras for taking me on an unforgettable tour of Italy in high school and inspiring the setting for this book.

CHAPTER ONE

Paying the Price

You may now turn on all electronic devices echoed through the intercom of the Boeing 747 as music to Carly's ears. After nine and a half hours of practicing her oboe fingerings on her pencil to the beat of Bertha Payne's snoring, she was ready to tear through the metal hull of the plane with her fingernails.

Carly turned on her phone and waited for her e-mails to load. As much as she loved her bff, Melody Mires, their friendship had taken a back seat to Melody's grand love affair with the conductor. Four seats up, Melody had glued her head to Wolf's shoulder. Carly and Melody had practically owned two seats at the bar of the Neighborhood Grill, which they'd frequented every night after rehearsal. Then Wolf showed up and bam! Girls' nights out ended for life. That left Carly with sweet, little old Bertha.

Her inbox flashed before her eyes in a horror show. Two hundred and seven e-mails. She couldn't remember the last time her phone had been shut off for so long.

Scrolling down, she hoped she hadn't missed anything too important. A few gig requests for last-minute summer weddings, three oboe students wishing her good luck on her Italian tour, and a whole ton of e-mails about her contemporary music group, *Women Reeds*. Although nothing was pressing, she'd had to pass on two concerts with other orchestras, three days of teaching, and a few wedding gigs.

Her best bet was to get through this tour and get back to the States as soon as possible so no one thought of her *missing in action* and started hiring her rivals.

Her finger stopped on a message from Dino Daywood, the DJ contractor who got her the swankiest gigs. *Last-minute performance request at the Hyatt Harborside. Tomorrow at noon. Show up and play Pachelbel's Canon. Twice union wages.*

Dammit! Hadn't she told him she'd be stranded in the Italian countryside for two weeks?

Wolf stood up from his seat beside Melody and cleared his throat. 'Attention all Easthampton Civic Symphony members. Welcome to Italy.' His thick German accent commanded their attention.

He smiled and straightened his broad shoulders, looking like a Roman gladiator. As much as Carly missed her friend, Melody really had scored big time. 'Our tour guide will be meeting us right outside the gate. His name is Michelangelo Ricci, a native from Tuscany and—get this—his family owns a vineyard. He's the best tour guide around and has been conducting tours since he was a young boy.'

As Carly squirmed in her seat, Wolf gestured to the orchestra's biggest donor and the board of directors. 'Ms. Maxhammer handpicked him after a series of rigorous interviews. Michelangelo knows his way around and will be with us every step of the way.' Wolf waved his hand over to the front of the plane, where people had already started pulling down their bags in first class. 'Play well and I hope you and your families enjoy the tour.'

Carly glanced at Bertha. By the time she woke up, they'd be the last ones off the plane. She needed to get to a quiet place and call Dino back. He wouldn't be happy, but he'd be even *less* happy if she didn't give him enough time to find someone else.

Carly's neck burned with frustration. Twice union wages, and a contact with the Hyatt Harborside. She'd been dreaming of playing there ever since she saw it glisten from across the Back Bay. *Enjoy your trip, my ass.*

She nudged the old violinist. 'Bertha, it's time to wake up.'

Al chuckled from the seat behind them as he picked up his trombone. He insisted his instrument have its own ticket, whereas Carly's oboe fitted in the overhead. 'There's only one way to wake her up.'

He unzipped his case and brought out his mouthpiece.

Carly shook her head. 'You're not going to—'

Before she could finish, Al buzzed the mouthpiece down by Bertha's ear.

Carly winced as Bertha's eyes flickered open. She smacked her dentures together and gazed up at Carly. 'We're there already?'

Al winked as he passed them down the aisle. 'You can thank me later.'

Carly gave him a dirty look. *In his dreams.* Melody may have made a lucky match in the orchestra, but Carly didn't mix business with pleasure. Her life was one hundred percent business and she endeavored to keep it that way.

It took forever to help Bertha with her violin and baggage. Only then did she have the luxury of whipping out her phone. Cringing, she dialed Dino's number and punched in his extension.

The other orchestra members gathered around the glass windows at the front of the Leonardo da Vinci International Airport. A man with curly dark hair wearing a white cotton shirt waved them over. His back was turned, so she couldn't make out his face, but she bet it was chubby and dark with a long, oily mustache like the guy on her pasta label. *Oh great, that must be the Italian guide.*

'Dirty Dancing DJs, Dino speaking.' He sounded like he was in the other room, not four thousand miles away.

Maybe a little distance, in this case, is good.

'Hey, Dino. It's Carly.'

'Hey babe, what's happening? Did you get the good news?'

The orchestra started to leave through the double doors. Melody waved to her, but Carly waved her back. 'That's what I'm calling about. I'm in Italy for the next two weeks. I left you a message—'

'Italy? Damn, girl. How am I supposed to book you over there?'

'One of my orchestras is on tour, and I had to go to keep my full-time status. I'm sorry. I thought you got the message.'

He sighed, sounding more annoyed than sad. 'Well, I guess I have to find someone else.'

Someone else. Those two words cut to her gut like reed sharpeners. In the gig business, if you refused, you got bumped to the bottom of the list. Dirty Dancing DJs was like the music mafia. It controlled every event center from the coast to western Massachusetts. She could already hear his fingers clicking over the keyboard for more numbers.

Someone tugged on her sleeve and she yanked her arm back. *Melody has some guts coming to me now after ignoring me for the whole flight.* 'Just give me a sec,' she hissed while covering the phone.

Dino hung up, leaving her with a dead phone stuck to her ear. Carly stomped her foot as anger threatened to get the better of her. How long would it take to rise back to the top of his precious list? 'Asshole.'

There was that tug on her arm again, this time more insistent. Fury boiling inside her, she whirled around. 'I told you—'

A man who looked like he'd walked off a Giorgio Armani ad glowed before her, illuminated by the Italian sun shining through the windows behind him. Midnight hair rolled in waves around his ears, slicked back from his face with just the right amount of mousse. Thick, perfectly sculpted, dark eyebrows contrasted with smooth, olive skin. Blue eyes with a ring of amber around the center mesmerized her.

'Are you with the Easthampton Civic Symphony, signorina?'

He accented his words just like the cultured Italian men on the James Bond films she had watched growing up.

'Yes, I was just—' what was she doing? Carly's voice trailed off.

'May I introduce myself? I am Michelangelo Ricci, your tour guide.'

Their tour guide? Carly's stomach plummeted. She'd just made a bitchy fool of herself right in front of the man she'd have to spend the next two weeks with. Great. Or what do the Italians say? Bene.

Michelangelo stared in expectation at her with his beautiful blue-amber eyes. What did he want? Some sort of pat on the back? A kiss? *Stop daydreaming.* Carly blinked back to reality. 'Yes?'

'And you are?'

'Oh. Carly Davis.'

He extended his hand. 'Nice to meet you, Carly.'

She took his hand in hers and squeezed. He had a strong grip with rough calluses, maybe from working outside in the vineyard? *Boy, this guy was too good to be true.* Which was why she should stay the hell away.

He released her hand politely, if not a little too soon for her taste. '*Per favore*, follow me. The tour bus is just beyond the doors.'

'I know that.' She grabbed her oboe case. Her long, floral bohemian skirt caught on her Birkenstock, and she tumbled face-forward on top of her luggage. Her over-packed bag broke her fall, but it didn't stave off a humbling wave of embarrassment.

He reached for her arm, pulling her up. '*Mio dio*, are you all right?'

Why was she so *off* all of a sudden? Must have been the conversation with Dino. It couldn't possibly be the tall, dark and gorgeous hottie, who must think she was the biggest idiot ever to land in Italy.

'I'm fine, thank you.' Her fingers shook as she grabbed the handle of her rolling bag. 'Just a long flight, that's all.'

'I'm sure it was.' His eyes glanced to where the bus was parked, looking *very* unconvinced. He reached for her oboe case, of all things. 'May I help you?'

'Absolutely not.' She pulled her case back. He may be hot, but she wasn't about to trust him with her twelve grand rosewood Lorée. Embarrassment climbed its way into her cheeks until she was pretty sure her entire face was red as a ketchup bottle. Her pale skin didn't help. Even at her most calm, her cheeks always looked pink.

'*Va bene.*' He stiffened as though slightly offended, then stepped away from her and moved toward the double doors. 'If you'll come this way.'

Carly followed him to the tour bus, dragging her luggage behind her and feeling like she was unwittingly doing everything she could to tick off the one person she'd have to rely upon for the next two weeks.

Maybe it was for the best. She was dangerously attracted to him, and the last thing she needed was a distraction.

Off to a great start.

*****

Michelangelo Ricci trudged to the tour bus feeling as though he'd signed away the next two weeks of his life. *Fourteen days of* vivere l'inferno, *or as the silly Americans would say, a living hell.*

It was because of wealthy Americans he was here, scraping together a paycheck so they didn't build luxury condos on his family's winery. The irony of his situation cackled in his face.

What Ms. Maxhammer and the rest of the orchestra didn't know was the only tours he had ever conducted were on his own vineyard. His family's land had fallen to him a few years ago, and if he didn't earn money fast, it would be history. Applying to Ms. Maxhammer's ad was his only way out, even if he had to stretch the truth.

As if taking care of spoiled, lazy tourists wasn't enough, the embodiment of the All-American Girl following him to the tour bus already grated on his nerves. The crazy part was that if she hadn't been so rude, he would have thought her intriguingly attractive. Not many women in his part of the world had such white-blonde hair and pale skin, looking more like she walked out of a fairytale than an airplane. Her pale-blue eyes were gorgeous, but it was the sheer determination mixed with intense vulnerability within them that piqued his attention.

Who was she talking to and why was it so important? Usually he didn't meddle in the affairs of others, but overhearing her desperation made him want to jump in like a knight in shining armor. All the way up until the part where she called the man an asshole. This woman could fight for herself.

So why did he feel such an inclination to help her?

Must be the big paycheck waiting for him after the tour ended. It wouldn't solve his family's problems, but it would buy them more time.

They reached the bus, and he turned around, wondering if he should even ask to help her with her bag again. The way she recoiled, clutching the small case to her chest made him wonder if she had trust issues. The last thing he wanted to do was piss off one of the Americans on his first day. Ms. Maxhammer had explicitly asked for the utmost courtesy.

'Would you like some help, signorina?' He prepared himself for the worst.

Carly narrowed her eyes, which turned to ice in the midday sun. 'You can take *this* bag.' She pointed to the large, heavy one with wheels.

'Very well.' He bent down and gripped the handle. His muscles bunched as he picked it up. *Mio dio.* What was in here — rocks?

Of course, he didn't want her to see him strain. Gritting his teeth, he hefted the bag up the steps and onto the luggage shelf at the front of the bus. It hit the shelf, rattling all the other bags before settling.

Edda, the bus driver, who could have posed as his mother, turned around and spoke in Italian. 'Is she the last one?'

13

He wiped his forehead. 'Si.'

Carly followed him up the steps, still clutching the smaller case like a baby, with small, elegant fingers. She looked like a lost princess who had misplaced her carriage. A pang of compassion shot through his chest. The desire to scoop her up and comfort her overwhelmed him. *Remember how she told that person off on the phone? You don't want to become asshole number two.*

Michelangelo scanned the seats. Every one was full, except the one next to him. *Great, I'll have to put up with her all the way to the hotel.* He gestured toward the front seat. 'Ladies first.'

She glanced around nervously, as if she'd rather sit anywhere but there. Michelangelo adjusted his collar, feeling slightly offended. He'd offered to help her with her bags twice and lifted her colossal boulder of luggage to the shelf, and this is how she treated him! Usually women enjoyed his company.

He stated the obvious, trying not to sound annoyed. 'It is the only seat left.'

'Oh, right.' Carly slipped into the window seat and adjusted her flowery skirt.

Resisting the urge to glance over the way the light fabric fell around her legs, he took the seat next to her. The bus merged with traffic and turned onto Roma Fiumicino, the main highway that led into Rome. Sunswept green fields spread before them.

Remembering he was supposed to be describing the landmarks, Michelangelo brought out a crumpled note from his pocket. Holding it in the palm of his hand, where no one would see, he turned on the intercom. 'I'd like to welcome all the members of the Easthampton Civic Symphony. Per Ms. Maxhammer's request, I'll be announcing important landmarks along the way.'

He checked the note. 'To your left is Lago Traiano, an artificial lake built by Imperatore Traiano in 98—117 B.C. and used as a port in the time of Imperial Rome.'

Turning off the intercom, Michelangelo glanced longingly at the circle of pines. He'd taken the guided tour on a horse-drawn carriage with his father as a young boy. *If only he was still here, he'd think of a way to save the vineyard.*

He turned his attention back to Carly. Scrolling down a list of e-mails on her cell, she didn't even look up to see the lake, which sent a dagger of pain through his gut. *Stupid American, can't even appreciate the Italian countryside.* Would she stay on that thing the whole time and miss all the views?

Michelangelo sat beside her once again and tried an attempt at conversation.

'Is this your first time in Italy?'

Carly nodded as she checked off the boxes beside the e-mails and deleted a bunch. 'First and last.'

Wow, he'd not heard that before. No visitor he'd ever met didn't want to come back. What was with her? Want stirred in his gut as he looked her up and down.

'Is that so? I'll have to change that.' The words slipped out of his mouth as more of a challenge than a remark. Did he just hit on her? What was getting into him?

Carly dropped her phone and glanced at him with a mix of surprise and dismay, and maybe—if he didn't imagine it—a hint of desire. She shifted a little further away, pressing her side against the window. 'Excuse me?'

Michelangelo's friends said he was smoother than gelato. He could work his way out of this. He shrugged. 'Everyone falls in love with Italy. Once you're here, you'll always remember it.'

'Besides music, I haven't fallen in love with anything in my entire life.' Carly twirled a strand of silky hair behind her ear. 'Good luck.'

Michelangelo took that as a challenge. Whether to make her fall in love with Italy, or with him, he wasn't sure.

15

CHAPTER TWO

Diva's Choice

Carly hoped Michelangelo couldn't see her heart beating like a metronome on *vivace*. She read the next e-mail, trying to focus and ignore how the hottie tour guide may have just hit on her.

Honestly, she must have read him completely wrongly, because they'd had about the worst introduction she could think of, and she'd watched a whole ton of romantic comedies in her day with Melody; *While You Were Sleeping, Groundhog Day, Pretty Woman, How to Lose a Guy in Ten Days*. She could go on and on—they'd even come up with their own top-fifty list.

Wait a sec. Didn't they all have rough starts?

Michelangelo leaned over and his eyes glanced down as if reading over her shoulder.

Sighing, she shut the screen off. She'd have to wait until they reached the hotel if she wanted any form of privacy.

'How long is this trip?' Her tone came out more annoyed than she would have liked. All the unread e-mails, the conversation with Dino, and her embarrassing introduction to Michelangelo had raised her anxiety to momentous levels. Thank the hotel gods for mini bars.

'It will take us about thirty minutes to reach the center of Rome, where the Villa Borghese is located.'

Great. Thirty minutes of spine-cringing awkwardness.

She turned to the window. Lush hills spread before her in blankets of emerald, accented by pointed, dark shrubs and patches of red and white wildflowers. An old farmhouse made with bleached stucco and red-orange tiled roofs claimed the side of a hill. Italy really was gorgeous.

Her phone vibrated with another new message.

Too bad she couldn't appreciate it.

Michelangelo gestured to her phone. 'You're a wanted woman.'

'Right now I am. Give it two weeks, and we'll see if they still call.' Carly tucked her cell in the front pocket of her purse, wishing she could control her mouth. Why was she spouting her problems to this man?

Michelangelo pouted his thick, velvety lips, a look which came across as sultry and alluring. 'You've got some fickle friends.'

She forced herself to stop staring at his lips and focused on his two-tone, blue-amber eyes. 'It's the nature of the bizz I'm afraid.'

'Sounds as risky as owning a vineyard.'

Oh yeah, right. Wandering through the vineyard and taste-testing great wines. Like he could really compare all the competition, the hours spent practicing, the expensive instruments, and the twenty-four-seven gig schedule? She crossed her arms and turned toward him. 'What do you mean?'

'The crop yield all depends on weather, pests, and the quality of the vines. One late frost, swarm of aphids, or disease can mean thousands lost. And that's just the beginning. Even if you have a good yield, you have to protect against bacteria, make sure the tanks are all sanitized, and check the bottling line systems and drainage systems. There's always something that needs fixing or replacing.' For a moment he looked older than his years—which couldn't be any more than hers.

Carly tried to lighten the mood. 'No wandering through the

18

vines drinking Chardonnay?'

Michelangelo laughed and looked at her as if he wished there was, just so they could do it together. 'More like being knee-deep in grape must or crawling into the tanks to sanitize them.'

Carly batted her eyelashes. 'How romantic.'

'You're telling me.' Michelangelo grinned.

OMG did I just flirt?

It had been a few years since she'd thrown herself out there, and she blushed like a giggly schoolgirl. Geez, she had to pull herself together or she'd end up on some crazy fling. Like that would last longer than the two-week tour.

Carly turned back to the window to cool things off, and they rode in silence.

The rolling hills had morphed into beige, white and pink stucco buildings interspersed with grand stone facades in the arched and domed architecture characteristic of Rome. Carly marveled at the bustling, narrow streets. The farthest she'd traveled was Disneyland in Florida as a kid. The absence of Starbucks, McDonald's, and any other US clothing and food chains gave the city a timeless, classic look.

I'm not in Kansas anymore.

The intercom buzzed as Michelangelo turned it on. He opened his hand, then closed it again and stuffed his palm into his pocket. Was he nervous? After all the tours he must have given, this should be old school for him.

Michelangelo took a deep breath. 'Up ahead we'll cross the Tiber river, which is the third-longest river in Italy. It comes from the Apennine Mountains in Emilia-Romagna and flows four hundred and six kilometers through Umbria and Lazio to the Tyrrhenian Sea. The king Tiberinus Silvius was said to have urinated in the river, which was subsequently renamed in his honor.'

Carly laughed out loud, then covered her mouth.

Michelangelo raised a dark eyebrow in question as he turned the intercom off and sat back down.

19

'Men. They have to mark their territory.'

He widened his gorgeous eyes. 'Is this how you view all men?'

Somehow, Carly felt as though he'd use her answer to judge every single thing about her character and whether she was available or not. It had to be good. And firm. It had to draw the line between them.

'Only the ones I've met so far.' Carly's heart sped. Why the hell would she say that? It was practically an invitation. Somewhere between America and Italy she'd lost her brain filter, and her mind.

'I see.' Michelangelo smiled as though he had a tasty secret on his luscious lips and gazed at the road ahead. Carly tried not to notice the way the fabric of his cotton shirt lay against his smooth chest, or the strength of his jawline.

They passed over the glassy Tiber river, and into downtown Rome. Residents watered their plants on the balconies and set up their storefronts under bright awnings. Carly could see why Michelangelo claimed everyone that visited wanted to come back. The city charmed her on a grand scale while still claiming its historic roots with pride.

The bus pulled up in front of a stone building with arched windows and striped, rounded awnings that reminded her of fancy candy wrappers. A red carpet lined the path to double glass doors. Carly breathed with relief. The air between them had grown thick with tension, and she was eager to get off the bus, get a drink and read her e-mail.

Michelangelo stood and addressed the entire bus. 'Welcome to the Villa Borghese. I'll see to it your luggage is deposited at your room. You may go directly to the front desk and check in.'

Carly stretched her legs and stood. She'd been sitting down all day, first on the plane, then on the bus and it felt good to move around. While Michelangelo helped people with their bags and answered questions, she took the opportunity to sneak away.

'Have a good stay, signorina.' A hint of playfulness danced in his voice.

She whirled around. Michelangelo smiled and winked, then turned to the rest of the orchestra. Feeling as though cupid's arrow had hit her straight through the head, Carly stepped off the bus and walked the red carpet into the Villa Borghese.

A white marble floor with lightning streaks of mica and gray spread out before her. Wooden columns, much like those in Roman architecture, structured the lobby area where two young men in crisp suits waited for her to check in. Both of them were handsome, dark Italian men, but neither compared to the one she'd just met.

Carly walked up to the main desk wondering who'd be sharing her room. A scandalous thought of Michelangelo in his boxers passed through her mind before she squelched it. *No, probably more along the lines of snoring Bertha.*

The man at the counter gave her a room key for three fifty-two. 'The elevator is around the corner to your right.' He spoke in perfect English. 'Welcome to the Villa Borghese.'

'Thank you. I mean, *grazie*.' Carly smiled. 'One more thing, who's staying with me?'

He checked his computer. 'Alaina Amaldi.'

Carly's heart froze over. *Not the diva who accused her of playing her high A two cents sharp!* 'There must be a mistake.'

He checked again, but not before giving her that *I think this lady is crazy* look. 'No, signorina. There is a specific request to place you two together.'

Dammit, Melody, you had to fall in love!

'I can assure you, I didn't place such a request.'

The host shook his head. '*Mi dispiace, signorina*. Perhaps Signorina Amaldi did?'

Carly shook her head. It was more likely their stage would freeze over and the curvy Alaina Amaldi would fall through it than the opera star would choose to room with her.

'Can't you change it?' *To Michelangelo.* She bit her tongue. 'How about Bertha Payne. Who's she staying with?' Anyone was better than that vibrato-crazed soprano.

He typed a few keys. 'I have her with Trudy Phillip. Per her request.'

Trudy, of course. She and Bertha were both as old as ancient Rome. They probably wanted to reminisce about the Coliseum days while they knitted doilies.

The line was lengthening behind her, and the receptionist flicked his eyes over the crowd nervously. Carly knew when she'd outstayed her welcome. 'Very well.' She adjusted her purse strap and followed his direction to the elevator.

This day is getting better and better.

CHAPTER THREE

Never-ending Songs

'May I?' Michelangelo offered his arm to the sweet little old lady who was the last orchestra member left on the bus. As he had helped the others with their bags, she sat knitting as though patiently waiting for him to come over.

'Of course, love.' She wrapped her knobbly hand around his arm. 'An old lady like myself will get whatever help she can.'

'You're like a fine Pinot Grigio, aged to perfection.' He kissed the tips of his fingers. 'Mmawh.' He helped her stand and walked to the front of the bus.

'I like you. What was your name again?' She squinted at him through glasses so thick they must have been bulletproof.

'Michelangelo.' He smiled as he took the last bag on the shelf, along with a violin case. He helped her down the steps and onto the sidewalk. 'And your name is?'

'Bertha, but my friends call me Bert.'

He kissed the back of her hand. 'Nice to meet you, Bert.'

'Oh the young ladies will like you.' She chuckled and walked away muttering to herself. 'Kissing my hand like I was a marriage prospect.'

Michelangelo stood with a pile of bags, wondering what had just happened in the last crazy hour of his life. Sure, in his opinion they were all self-centered, ill-mannered, brash-speaking Americans, but they also had an openness to them he was beginning to like.

Carly was another story.

Two concierges came through the double glass doors with carts, and he helped them load the luggage while immersed in his thoughts. Why had he told her about his winery? He had sworn not to tell any of them the real reason why he was doing this tour for fear Ms. Maxhammer would see right through the elaborately constructed façade. And, of course, the only tours he'd ever led were on his own vineyard. He had no idea what he was doing. He was in it for the money, and the money alone.

A little voice inside him teased, *what about Carly?*

Her witty comebacks had impressed him, and every moment they sat together, the chemistry rose until he thought the air around them would explode into fireworks before they reached the hotel.

'We're to deliver these to the assigned rooms, signore?' The boy reminded him of himself ten years ago when he was lifting barrels on the vineyard. So much responsibility had been put upon him since then.

'Si, si.' He handed them a list of the names and room assignments. 'Pronto!'

The boys scurried off. The lists! He slapped his hand over his face. He'd just given them his way of contacting Carly.

You're better off forgetting about her and doing your job.

Ms. Maxhammer had hired him to be polite, not to seduce the members of her orchestra. If she found out anything had happened, it would be scandalous. She might even fire him, and he needed that check.

Still, his chest stirred with desire. The last time a woman had caught his attention this badly had been years ago. After college, when his father had grown ill, he'd thrown all his energy into working on his vineyard. Dating was a lost memory.

Maybe it's time to get out and look around. That little voice hounded him again. This time it was more insistent.

Casually, Michelangelo walked to the desk. One of the receptionists greeted him. *'Ciao, signore.'*

'Ciao, signore' He leaned on the marble countertop. 'Are all of my guests accounted for?'

'Si. They were all eager to get to their rooms after such a long trip.'

'Eccellente.' Michelangelo ran his hands through his hair. 'Do you mind if I have a look at the list? The baggage boys took mine.'

The host paused, and for a bleak second Michelangelo thought he'd turn him down. He offered more of an explanation, hoping he didn't look too desperate. 'Just to verify your list with the bus roster.'

'Ma certo, signore.' He turned the computer screen toward Michelangelo.

Michelangelo scanned the names, nodding along the way to assure the receptionist that everything matched up. 'All the names are there.' His eyes stopped on Carly Davis, room three fifty-two. He committed the number to memory. Just in case. *'Grazie.'*

'Anytime.' As the man moved to turn the computer back, Michelangelo read Carly's roommate: Alaina Amaldi.

Merda! A memory of the diva requesting her own private limousine instead of the bus came to mind. She'd grumble to Ms. Maxhammer if he so much as touched her doorknob. Out of all the people on the tour why did Carly's roommate have to be her?

Maybe fate was telling him to leave Carly alone and do his damn job. His vineyard needed him, and he refused to break the last link in the family chain. He wanted to pass the lands down to his sons, and his grandsons and great grandsons for years to come. He wasn't about to let some fling ruin his plan.

Yet, as he checked into his own room, the number still resurfaced in his mind like a song that never ended.

Carly Davis. Room three fifty-two.

Carly plopped onto the hotel bed and closed her eyes. There was no sign of Alaina, so the diva's limousine must have run into problems along the way—which was fine with her. She needed time to check her e-mails and forget about the sexy conversation she had had with Michelangelo.

How his eyes zeroed in on her as if she were the only woman on the bus.

How his legs had brushed against hers.

Enough! She dug out her phone and brought up her e-mails. *Finally some time to catch up.*

The door burst open and a curvy young woman with hair bright as fire wearing a sequined, fluorescent-green Versace miniskirt waltzed in. The concierge followed her, with a parade of white leather Louis Vuitton luggage.

She glanced at Carly and sighed as if she'd had the worst day ever. 'Why does Italy have to be so damned far away?'

Carly shrugged. Even though she'd been thinking something similar, she wasn't going to respond to such an egocentric statement. 'If you live here, it's pretty close.'

'Ugh!' Alaina rubbed her temples, then turned to the concierges still standing at the door like seals before a shark. 'Place them on the bed right side up.'

The boys did as they were told, and she handed them each five euros. At least she wasn't a cheap prima donna.

Carly stood, leaving her phone on her bed. 'There must be a mistake.'

'There's no mistake, Ms. Davis.' Alaina smiled, reminding Carly of an evil Disney queen. 'I specifically requested you so we could practice my aria. The last few rehearsals have been, shall I say… uninspired.'

Her words slapped Carly in the face. 'Excuse me?'

'This is my Italian debut, and I mean it to be fabulous. I already have three newspapers set up to provide quotes for my biography. Which reminds me—'

She unzipped one of the bags and pulled out a red, crystal-encrusted gown. 'Matching dresses! Although mine has a *tad* more bling because I am the star after all. Isn't it ingenious?'

Carly gawked at the sparkly, eye-bleeding fabric wondering how she'd squeeze her breasts in the plunging neckline, and then how she'd play her oboe in it. One bow too low was an immediate wardrobe malfunction. Not to mention being shown up by a voluptuous beauty.

As if Alaina could read her mind, she waved her concerns off. 'Don't worry; I had the dressmakers at Versace alter the fit to accommodate your stick figure. You'll have no problem slipping it on. So?' Alaina tapped her long, bright-red fingernails on the dresser.

Carly felt like a bird trapped in a tiny cage. If she gave Alaina any reason to complain, it could cost her points with Wolf, and Ms. Maxhammer. She knew the gig business enough to play the game. Never burn bridges. Contacts were the most important tool you could have. 'Okay, I'll try it on.'

'Wonderful!' Alaina clapped her hands. 'But only after we rehearse.'

Carly gave her phone one last longing glance. 'Right now?'

Alaina gave her a blank-eyed stare. 'Our first concert is tomorrow—the Coliseum, remember?'

The itinerary flashed through Carly's mind. She had only briefly peeked at it before the trip, but she did remember something about performing in the Coliseum. Funny how the last thing she wanted to play right now was an aria about a wedding. 'Oh, all right.'

Alaina warmed up with an ascending five-note pattern while Carly soaked her reed in her I-love-NY shot glass. She reminded herself to get one for her collection while in Italy.

They set up as though they were in concert, looking out the window at the darkening sky as the sun set over Rome. Carly started with the cheery oboe interlude of Bach's typical running eighth and sixteenth notes.

Alaina took a deep breath and came in right on cue.

Sich üben im Lieben,
In Scherzen sich herzen
Ist besser als Florens vergängliche Lust.

As Carly played, she thought of the translation, memorized long ago for a music history exam of the Baroque Period. For the first time since she'd practiced the aria all the way back in her New England Conservatory days, the meaning came through:

To become adept in love,
to jest and caress
is better than Flora's passing pleasure.

Yeah right. She took a deep breath and played through the next interlude before Alaina came back in. To become adept in love would give you one thing: distraction along with a big dose of heartbreak. It was so much more useful to put your time into something tangible that yielded better results, like classical music and her career. Bach had gotten the sentiment all wrong. Love was a passing pleasure, just like spring.

Alaina stopped singing and Carly realized the song had ended.

'Carly, what's wrong?' Alaina's face fell in true concern, which didn't happen very often.

Carly shrugged. She didn't want to put down Alaina's aria, but the soprano had asked for the truth. 'This is the silliest, most superficial song I've ever heard. I don't get the words. *Adept in love*? What does that mean, really?'

Instead of flaring up with anger, Alaina simply waved it off. 'It's just a song. He probably wrote it for some big commission. It doesn't matter what it means, it matters how you play it.' She took a sip of water and cleared her throat. 'It needs a little more energy, more mischievousness. One more time?'

Carly sighed, feeling like she'd hit her head against the wall. They could practice the aria as many times as Alaina wanted, but Carly couldn't play it wholeheartedly if she didn't believe what it said. She could pretend, but the best of the best would sense her reserve.

'Sure.' She felt like a broken record playing the song that never ended. *Second verse, same as the first…*

CHAPTER FOUR

Wandering Eyes

Sunlight streamed through the crack in the curtains, warming the back of Carly's hand. She rubbed her eyes, half stuck in her dream surrounded by jesting and caressing lovers while she lectured Bach on the finer points of writing song lyrics. In German.

Carly propped her head on her elbow. *I don't speak German.*

She reached out and pulled the curtains back, expecting her view of Boston's Back Bay. Instead, the bustling streets of Italy sprawled before her, interspersed with red-orange roofs and ancient stone. The tour. Michelangelo.

Dammit.

She checked her phone. Seven forty-five. They were supposed to be on the bus by eight for the soundcheck at the Coliseum.

Hadn't she set the alarm?

'Alaina.' She called over to the sleeping beauty in the bed beside her. 'Alaina wake up.'

Alaina turned on to her other side, exposing the lacy back of her silk nightgown and grumbled under her breath. 'More sleep.'

Carly sprang out of bed. 'We have to be at the bus in ten minutes.'

Alaina waved her off. 'They'll wait for us.'

Carly picked up her toiletries and stumbled to the shower. Wolf had hired a crew to film this concert for the local TV stations. There was no way she was going with dirty hair. 'I know I set my alarm.'

'I shut it off.' Alaina buried her head in her pillow.

'You what?' Carly stuck her head out from the bathroom door as the shower warmed up.

'I shut it off. Who wants to get up at seven a.m.?'

Note to self: next time, lock your phone. 'I do. That's when I play my long tones.' Even now she worried about how she'd reach high A without warming up.

Alaina held up a finger, the nail bright red. 'Precisely why I shut it off.'

Carly couldn't decide whether to jump in the shower or strangle the diva. Ultimately, clean hair was better than revenge. She tore off her pajamas and chose the shower.

Twenty minutes later, they approached the bus dragging Alaina's garment bag with the two matching dresses behind them. Orchestra members filled the seats. Every face stared at them from the windows as they approached. Some of them already wore their concert black, making Carly feel as though such a slouch in her Women Reeds t-shirt and skinny jeans.

'What happened to your limo?' Shame-faced and frazzled—which seemed to be the theme of this trip—Carly shielded her eyes from the bus. She hoped Michelangelo was *not* there to witness this next great embarrassing moment in her life.

'I fired him.' Alaina strutted in her fuchsia heels as thought she was walking the runway in her metallic miniskirt and halter top. She gestured toward the bus. 'See, I told you they'd wait for us.'

The doors to the bus unfolded.

Please, please, please let it be someone other than Michelangelo.

The Italian hottie jumped down the last two steps and smiled like he'd won a game. 'There you two are. We were starting to worry.'

Carly considered blaming Alaina, but thought better of it. He already thought she was a bitch. Better not make that a mega bitch.

'I'm sorry. We missed the alarm.' Carly handed him the garment bag.

He offered his hand to her, and Alaina stepped between them and took it instead. 'Thank you.'

'Mio Dio, signorina.' Michelangelo stepped back as if she'd attacked him. But, he recovered his charm quickly. 'You must be eager to start your tour?'

'Si.' Alaina grinned. 'But not without an escort.'

'I can take care of that.' Michelangelo escorted her up the steps.

Carly shook her head and followed behind them. Had she misinterpreted everything that had happened yesterday? Or was he just a big flirt?

As Alaina reached the top of the stairs, she waved to everyone on the bus as thought she was the Queen of England. Michelangelo glanced at Carly and winked.

Maybe he had thought of her after all. She noticed the front seat next to him wasn't taken. Had he saved it for her?

'I must ride in the front of the bus.' Alaina placed her hand over her heart. 'I suffer from severe motion sickness.'

Michelangelo paused, scanning the seats. His face tightened like a man who'd lost a hand of cards. 'Of course.'

He turned to Carly. 'My apologies, Ms. Davis. There is one seat open in the back if that will suit you.'

Severe disappointment flustered Carly and she pushed it back. *Why the hell do I care if she sits next to the tour guide?*

She pulled herself together as Ms. Maxhammer gave her a purposeful stare. Battling Alaina over a man wasn't worth her principal oboe seat. *Think of all the e-mails you'll get to answer without him.*

'Yes, that's fine.' Carly shuffled past them and walked down the aisle. Her gaze settled on the last empty seat, which was slam bam next to horny Al. He wore an old Bruins t-shirt with holes in the front. A Red Sox cap half-covered his oily hair.

He tapped the seat and grinned. 'Hey, babe. Looks like you're sitting with me.'

Carly resisted the urge to gag. Any man entertained by emptying his spit valve ranked a tad below the maturity line in her book. She tried anything to get away. 'Where's your trombone?'

He shrugged and pouted. 'They made me put her under the bus for safekeeping.'

'Bummer.' For both of them.

He smirked. 'I'd say there's a silver lining.'

She settled into her seat and whipped out her phone. Hopefully, Al would take the hint and leave her alone.

The bus started to move, and he turned to her. 'Sleep well last night?' The faint smell of cheap alcohol wafted from his lips.

Carly coughed a little in her throat. His question was innocent enough, but coming from him, it sounded sleazy—like he pictured her sleeping in the nude. She finished her e-mail before replying with the least-sexy answer possible. 'Like a brick.'

His gaze held expectation, but she wasn't going to ask about his nighttime escapades. Instead, she returned to her e-mails.

Al adjusted his baseball cap and leaned toward the window as though he got the picture.

Maybe he isn't so dense after all.

Carly had a few moments of pure e-mail answering bliss before her skin prickled on the back of her neck. The distinct feeling someone was watching her came over her. She glanced over to Al. He'd propped his head against the window and was sleeping like an oversized baby on Nyquil. *Probably too much late-night drinking with his brass buddies.*

Carly rolled her eyes. If all men were so simple-minded and easily entertained, she'd have no problem focusing on her career for the rest of her life. Never mind the distraction of dating and the sticky business of falling in love. She placed her hand on her oboe case. *You and me, girl. Foreva.*

The prickling sensation returned, and Carly casually glanced around the bus, trying not to weird anyone out. What did her

35

mom used to say? Something about if your necklace chain had turned around, someone was thinking about you. She touched the rhinestone G clef in the nape of her neck. The clasp had fallen to the front. *Interesting.*

Pretending to stretch her arms, Carly scanned the bus behind her. A few of the older violinists slept, the percussionist snapped pictures with his phone, and Melody and Wolf whispered in each other's ears.

How sweet. She loved her friend but seriously, if she'd had time for breakfast, she'd be hurling it up. Romance was not for her.

Carly moved to turn back around, but Melody caught her gaze. Her friend widened her eyes in a WTF look and pointed to the front of the bus behind the seat in front of her, where no one else could see.

So she caught the culprit, eh? Carly turned around slowly, not wanting to give herself away. Alaina was chatting like an energizer bunny at the front of the bus. But Michelangelo wasn't listening. Instead, he'd positioned his elbow over the seat, allowing him to turn in Carly's direction. As their eyes met, he gave her another sultry wink.

Carly dropped her gaze immediately, her cheeks turning into tomatoes. Two winks in one day? Who did he think she was? His secret cohort?

Behind her, Melody giggled. Carly guessed it wasn't something Wolf had said.

*****

Michelangelo prayed for the bus ride to end soon. Carly's sassy banter and reluctance to open up had intrigued him, but this opera diva's ongoing lecture about herself was as boring as a documentary on drainage pipes. Sure, Alaina Amaldi was magnificently pretty, but a challenging puzzle lured him more than a superficial prize.

'When I was only fifteen, my parents drove me to Juilliard to study with the famous Edith Bers, who gave the US premiere of Schumann's *Des Sängers Fluch*. She said my talent rivaled some of the great opera singers of our time.'

Michelangelo wished he could sneak another peek at Carly, but Ms. Maxhammer had already caught him glancing in the same direction three times. *Better to make the diva happy and bide my time.* 'Schumann, eh? Tell me more about your studies.'

Alaina took a deep breath as if she was about to hit a high note, and his phone vibrated in his pocket. 'Oh, one moment, per favore.'

She creased her perfectly sculpted eyebrows in consternation.

'This may concern the concert.'

She shifted in her seat. 'Oh, okay. Go ahead.'

He pulled out his phone and recognized the caller ID. Dread ate away at his boredom. Even though it wasn't about the concert, he had to take it.

'Pronto, Isabella. What can I do for you?'

'The real-estate agents are here again.' Her voice was hushed as if she muffled her mouth against the phone. 'They're eyeing the northern vineyards.'

Merda! Since the new American company took over their lease, all they'd ever wanted was to get them out of there. It seemed that condos overlooking a token vine patch in Tuscany were more profitable than a real winery. He balled his fist. 'Tell them they're going to have to talk to my lawyer.'

'But, signore, you don't have a lawyer.'

Oh right. That's what happens when you can't pay people anymore. As it was, he had no idea how long he could pay Isabella to manage the office. 'They don't know that. Tell them he'll be in contact in the next week or so. It will buy us some time.'

'Si, signore.' She sounded defeated, resigned. The weight in her voice dropped like a bomb in his heart.

He changed the subject, trying to cheer her up. 'How are the little ones?'

'Good. Anna can say bubblegum now, so that's all she talks

about. Camelia's fighting with her brother, like always, and the littlest one's kicking like he's on his way out!'

Michelangelo laughed, trying to imagine them all. 'Hopefully he'll wait another month, eh?'

'You know I can't control these things.' She sighed.

'And how's Rodolfo?'

'His back's feeling better. He's in the distillery moving crates now.'

'Good. Glad to hear it.' Isabella's family had been working for the vineyard even since he was a little boy. He needed to give her some hope she wouldn't have to relocate. 'I'll be back in two weeks, and I'll have more than enough to keep the real-estate sharks at bay for a while. Then I can figure out how to purchase the whole property so this won't happen again.'

Sure, it's as simple as a few thousand euros. That's all.

'*Va bene, signore*.' Isabella's sweet voice rung a little more cheerfully.

'Hang in there. Send my well wishes to Rodolfo.' He hung up, feeling as though the weight of the bus rested on his shoulders. So many workers relied on him, and he couldn't disappoint his father, may he rest in peace.

Michelangelo buried his face in his hands and massaged his forehead with his fingers.

'What was all that about?' Alaina's penetrating voice woke him up. He'd forgotten all about her.

Mio Dio. Would I have to explain all my problems to her? Not that she'd listen. Then, he realized the whole conversation had been in Italian. So many Americans only spoke English. However, Ms. Amaldi was a vocalist, trained to sing in multiple languages. He appraised her. 'Are you fluent in Italian, signorina?'

She squirmed in her seat as if he'd asked her what her grades were in trigonometry. 'German and French are my specialties.'

She must suck at Italian. Thank God.

He waved it off. 'Just something about a family matter. It's not important.'

'Well, as I was saying…' She continued as if she'd already forgotten about his call. 'After high school, I was accepted at both Juilliard and the New England Conservatory. Let me tell you, that was a tough decision.'

Out of the corner of his vision, he saw the stone arches of the Coliseum and breathed with relief. 'Oh look! What do you know? We're here already!'

As the members of the orchestra stood and took pictures, Michelangelo consulted his notes. The conversation with Isabella had shaken him, and he had trouble focusing on all of the details. Sure, he knew some things from his schooling, but exact dates and names stayed in the murky area of his memory. He'd much rather be pruning his grapevines.

Ms. Maxhammer gave him an encouraging look, and he nodded and turned on the intercom. 'The Coliseum was built in—' he coughed, 'AD 72 under the emperor…Vespasian and was completed in AD 80 under Titus.'

Isn't there something in my notes about the original name?

He glanced at Ms. Maxhammer, who watched him with interest. He couldn't sneak another peak at his notes, so he bought some time with what he did know. 'Contrary to popular thought, the movie *Gladiator* was not filmed here. Most of those images were computer-generated.'

A few members of the orchestra chuckled, enjoying his momentary excursion into popular culture, but Ms. Maxhammer pursed her lips and tapped her fingers on the top of the bus seat. *She had probably never seen it.* He should have made reference to 1950s movies like *Julius Caesar* and *Cleopatra*.

Then his memory came back to him in a rush of relief. 'Originally called the Flavian amphitheatre, it is the largest ever built in the Roman Empire, made of concrete and stone. Capable of seating fifty thousand spectators, it is considered one of the greatest works of Roman architecture.'

The doors opened, and Michelangelo jumped out to help unload the larger instruments from the storage space underneath the bus. Hopefully, they'd arrived intact. He'd sworn his life away convincing the musicians to store them there in the first place. One dent and he'd have a problem for the rest of the trip.

He opened the storage compartment and prayed. Cases had shifted during the short ride to the center of town, but nothing looked damaged or out of place. As the orchestra members filed off the bus, he started with the cellos first.

He had to pull things together. He'd be a pretty lousy tour guide if his vineyard troubled him too much to recount the exact dates and details from his notes. If he couldn't think straight enough to conduct the tour, than he wouldn't get the big check at the end.

After he set up the orchestra and made sure everyone was happy, he'd consult his program notes. As translator, he'd have to announce the Easthampton Civic Symphony in both Italian and English, and he wanted to make an impression on Ms. Maxhammer.

He checked the compartment. Three instruments were left, along with some percussion equipment. He brought out two violins and turned to see Carly waiting for him.

'Signorina! I trust you had a pleasant ride?' Even though he flashed his most charming smile, he went into panic mode. There were no oboes under the bus. Had he lost her instrument?

Carly placed a hand on her hip. 'I got a lot done, but I wouldn't exactly call it pleasant.'

He glanced back at the almost-empty storage compartment and his stomach hollowed. Why else would she come to him if she already had her instrument? 'It seems your oboe is…'

'Right here.' She turned to the side, showing off her square black bag.

Relief trickled over him. 'Snuck it on, did you?'

She grinned, looking like a mischievous pixie as the sunlight brought out the freckles on her nose. 'I have my ways.'

So, if she wasn't here for her instrument, what was she here for? Michelangelo leaned toward her, wondering if his flirtatious tactics had worked. 'I wonder what those are.'

She stepped back, her face turning into a professional mask. 'I'm picking up a trombone for Al Greenwood. The case should be black.'

Was that the man she'd sat next to? A current of jealousy rippled through him, even though he had no claim on her at all. Seems he had some competition. 'He can't pick it up for himself?' What was with these American men? Was there no sense of chivalry?

Carly scratched her forehead above her left eye as if considering what to say, which only piqued his interest more.

She leaned over and whispered in his ear. 'Let's just say he had a little too much fun last night and is searching for a bathroom as we speak.'

'Oh, I'm sorry to hear that.' So Carly liked the party boys? Somehow he had a hard time believing that.

Michelangelo reached in and brought out the case with Al's name on it. He handed it to her, their fingers brushing. Heat traveled up his hand to his shoulder.

Carly looked away. Either she'd felt it too and couldn't handle it, or she felt nothing at all. She turned toward the main entrance of the Coliseum.

A cord tugged on his heart, as if she'd lured him in with a fish hook and hadn't let him free. Michelangelo wasn't ready to say goodbye. 'Ms. Davis?'

She whirled around, swinging the trombone in the air. 'Yes?'

He pointed to the grand arches behind them. 'What do you think?'

She wrinkled her perfect little button nose and shrugged. 'Looks old and crumbly to me.'

Before he could respond, she'd turned back to join the rest of the orchestra.

Michelangelo laughed, his mood lifted from the earlier call. *Ah, how I've missed Carly's sass.*

CHAPTER FIVE

A Chance in the World

The rehearsal and soundcheck dragged on forever. Sure, it was neat to play where Roman gladiators had once battled to the death almost two thousand years ago. But the newness wore off pretty quickly, turning into two hours of measure counting. To make matters worse, Wolf had crammed the orchestra into the part of the Coliseum where the tourists could walk, because the rest of the structure was too old and too precious. She had no idea where the audience would sit. There was so little space as it was that the back row of violas threatened to impale her with their every up-bow.

Not that a whole bunch of Italian people were going to drop their normal routine on a Wednesday and come watch an orchestra during their lunch break.

Forty-nine-two-three-four, fifty-two-three-four. Her mind wandered to Michelangelo. Putting down his country's most famous iconic landmark was downright mean. He was a tour guide, for crying out loud. He must love ancient history. She vowed to apologize and find something nice to say the first chance she got.

Melody elbowed her from her principal flute's seat. 'Sixty-two!'

Carly blinked in surprise. She must have lost count, which hadn't happened to her since her high school orchestra days. Sticking her way-too-dry reed into her oboe, she hoped the first few notes would come out.

Wolf gave her the cue, and she took a deep breath. Her first note came out like the squawk of a duck. Mortified, she adjusted the air stream and the pressure behind the sound, smoothing over the next set of notes.

Cursing Alaina for not letting her play through her long tones, she finished her solo with a sweet taper and breathed. She wouldn't admit it was because of her own preoccupation with a certain tour guide. No way in hell.

Wolf held the last fermata in a glorious swell of sound, ending the song.

He placed both hands on the podium and his blue-eyed gaze scanned the orchestra, settling on Carly. A muscle twitched in his temple, making her anxiety level spike.

Oh no, here it comes.

'Excellent job, my friends. We will give this audience something to remember.' Wolf closed his score with finality.

Carly let go of a breath she didn't realize she'd been holding. Maybe losing your bff to the conductor had its advantages? He was less inclined to pick at her mistakes. Still, Carly missed her time with Melody. She'd rather be called out than have to sit with Bertha and Al.

Wolf grinned, bringing out the harsh angles of his German face. 'I have a treat in store for you. Our fabulous tour guide has arranged a picnic lunch right here in the Coliseum. He's ordered some of Italy's finest meats, cheeses, and breads. Please help your-self and have a breather. We are scheduled to be back on stage, dressed and ready to play by one o'clock.'

The orchestra muttered in agreement and began packing up. Carly opened her case and ran her lucky cleaning rag over her oboe.

'Are you okay?' Melody leaned over as she polished her flute.

45

Carly furrowed her eyebrows, feeling like a five-year-old who'd bruised her knee. 'I'm perfectly fine, why?'

Melody shrugged sheepishly. 'You never miss entrances. Usually you're the one that helps me come in.'

'Must be the jet lag. I'm still getting used to the fact that it's still sunny at midnight.'

'Yeah, that is strange, isn't it?' Melody closed her case and stood, stretching her legs.

'Eating with Wolf?' Carly tried not to sound jealous.

'Actually, he had a meeting with Ms. Maxhammer so I was hoping…' Melody batted her dark eyelashes. 'You'll take me back.'

'I don't know. I was really looking forward to talking about World War Two with Bertha and Trudy.'

Melody laughed. 'What have I done to you?'

Carly smiled and waved her away, feeling like the old Melody had returned. 'Made me get out of my bubble, that's what you've done. I had to join the world sometime.'

'True, but how about a little reminiscing?' Melody waved to Wolf, then turned back to her.

Carly winked. 'Only if we get to gossip.'

Melody hiked her flute bag over her shoulder. 'Boy, do I have some fodder for you, and a few questions of my own.'

Carly's heart dropped to the stage. Would Melody ask about Michelangelo's wandering eye? If she backed out now that would certainly make the matter worse. 'All right. But I can't promise anything too juicy.'

Melody pushed her music stand down. 'You don't have to promise anything at all.'

Michelangelo was nowhere to be seen when they approached the table with all of the packed lunches. Guilt panged Carly's chest. She still had to apologize to him. But not here, not in front of Melody. Her friend would take that one little *I'm sorry* and run with it, making something grand out of nothing at all.

Or, at least she thought it was nothing.

They picked up two mini picnic baskets and found a quiet spot outside the Coliseum on the grass. Carly gazed up at the part where the delicate carvings on the top broke off into the arches below. The shadowy stone gave her the creeps, as if ghosts of spectators lurked in the depths.

Not that she believed in ghosts. But she refused to live in any apartment building older than fifty years. Just in case.

Melody smeared some cheese over a slice of focaccia. 'Someone's got the hots for you.'

Carly almost spat out the grape she'd just stuffed into her mouth. 'What?'

'You know who I'm talking about.' Melody jabbed her finger behind her. 'Mr. Tour Guide.'

Carly tried to look surprised. 'Why do you think that?'

'Because he was ogling you the whole trip here. Not to mention how interested he looked sitting next to you yesterday.'

'It's his job to make us comfortable.' She half-convinced Melody and half-convinced herself.

'Yeah, but he didn't have a smidgen of the enthusiasm he had with you when talking with Alaina.'

Carly tightened her lips to resist smiling as satisfaction rippled through her. *Yeah, take that, diva supreme.* She remembered she was supposed to be fighting him off and shrugged as if she didn't care. 'Just another flirt.'

'He's actually pretty darn gorgeous.' Melody sighed and shook her head. 'Too bad, if you ask me. Not only does he live a world away, but he's not even a musician. I mean, what the heck would you do on a vineyard?'

Carly shrugged and stuffed another grape into her mouth. The problem was, she could think of more than a few things to do.

Melody frowned as if Carly's aversion to the tour guide was a truly tragic thing. 'He doesn't have a chance with you.'

'You got that right.' Carly finally felt as though they'd wandered back into safe territory. 'My life's so full; I can't imagine squeezing another thing into it. Something would have to give, and I'm telling you now it's not my career.'

A mischievous look danced in her friend's eyes. She brushed her hands on her black pants and stood. 'Maybe I should just go over and tell him to forget it, so he doesn't waste his time.'

'Don't you dare!' Carly grabbed her friend's arm.

Melody's eyes widened as though she'd caught her in a trap. 'Why's that?'

Absolute mortification zapped through Carly. Not only would it bring attention to the fact they'd been talking about him, but she wasn't ready to blow him off like that. She still had an apology to make.

Melody waited for a reasonable response, tapping her toe.

Carly had to come up with something quickly. The truth was, she didn't know him all that well. He seemed flirtatious and bold, like a Casanova. She narrowed her eyes. 'Something tells me he'll take that as a challenge.'

'You're probably right.' Melody settled down again next to her and winked. 'Wouldn't want that, would we?'

Carly popped a chunk of blue-veined, crumbly cheese in her mouth. She needed to change the subject quickly before she said something she shouldn't. 'So how are you and Wolf?'

Melody placed her hand on her lacy, silk blouse over her heart. 'We just had our one-year anniversary.'

The cheese left a sour taste on Carly's tongue, which was totally canceled out by Melody's sweet answer. Even though she missed her friend, she was happy for her. 'Great.'

'Here's the gossip I promised you…' Melody twirled a strand of her dark, curly hair around her finger. 'He's hinted at a ring.'

'A ring!' To Carly, that would be like a death sentence for all her dreams. Hopefully, Melody would take her shocked expression as a happy surprise and not horror. 'You don't think you're moving too fast?'

Melody sighed. 'I'm not like you. Sure, I love music, but I want more to my life; a happy marriage, maybe a family. The truth is, I've been looking to settle down with someone for a while now. I just haven't told you because I didn't want you to freak out.'

'Like I'm doing now?' Carly laughed, relieved that Melody had finally decided to confide in her. She'd known something was up ever since her friend started spewing melancholy reflections about life on their drinking nights after concerts.

'To tell *you* the truth, I thought Wolf might be a phase, and we'd get together again after the whole whirlwind romance ran its course. But, I was wrong.' *Boy, did that come out the wrong way.* Carly raised her hand. 'Thank goodness I was wrong—because you too seem very happy together, and I want you to be happy…' She realized she was rambling and stopped as shame burned in her cheeks.

Instead of being angry, Melody reached over and squeezed her hand. 'It's my fault. I shouldn't have abandoned you like I did, spending all my free time with him. I got a little obsessed. I promise, when we get back, I'm going to carve out time for us.'

A wall crumbled in Carly's heart. Those words were the best thing she'd heard ever since landing in Italy. 'I'd like that.'

'That's if you don't find a whirlwind romance of your own.' Melody's gaze focused upon something behind Carly's right shoulder, in the direction of the entrance to the Coliseum. 'Speak of the devil.'

Nervous jitters danced up Carly's arms. 'No way.'

'Yup, straight off a Valentino ad.'

Carly brushed the crumbs off her shirt and stashed the remainder of her lunch in her picnic basket. She wouldn't want him thinking she was a pig on top of a lazy, bossy, profanity-laced oboe witch.

'Good afternoon, signorine.'

'Hey there, Michelangelo.' A hint of amusement tinged Melody's voice, which Carly hoped he didn't pick up on.

Calmly turn around. Pretend nothing has happened—because

nothing really had. But, when Carly turned around, there was nothing calm about her. Michelangelo had changed into a crisp, black tux with a silver vest and tie, which brought out his stone-hard physique. A waft of pine and citrusy aftershave blew by on the wind, tantalizing her senses. She had the distinct urge to run her hands through his long curls.

Stop it! Why was he crashing their girls' lunch? Didn't men understand some things were private?

As if reading her mind, he gestured toward the entranceway. 'I was told to round up the last stragglers. Maestro Braun wants everyone changed into concert attire.' He eyed Carly's t-shirt and skinny jeans up and down, lingering a little too long on her legs.

'What time is it?' Melody shot up, eyes bright with alarm.

He checked his phone. 'Twelve thirty-eight. The concert is in twenty minutes.'

Carly swallowed a rising current of embarrassment. Again. *Great. Late for the coach this morning and now this. He thinks I'm totally time-challenged.*

'Geez, where did all the time go?' Melody collected the last of her things and started running to the entrance. 'See ya there, chico. I still need to organize my music!'

Michelangelo smiled at Carly. Sure, a few long tones would make her job easier. But now was her chance to apologize. It would only take a few seconds more.

'Listen, about that comment I made about the Coliseum—'

He took her hand, sending tingling zaps of warmth from her fingers to her toes. 'Don't apologize.'

'But I—'

'Shhh.' His calloused finger touched her lips, seizing her heart. 'I liked it.'

CHAPTER SIX

Vision in Red

Michelangelo pressed his finger to Carly's velvety lips, wishing his lips were there instead. It was so sweet of her to apologize for her joke about the Coliseum. As though he was that sensitive? *Bring it on, signorina.* Having a name like *Michelangelo* warranted jokes far above and beyond a crumbly old stadium.

Carly stepped back and picked up her oboe case and her picnic basket. 'I have to go.'

'Of course. Wouldn't want you to be late.' He smiled, and an adorable blush rose in her cheeks.

Carly averted her eyes. 'I'm already late.' Without a backward glance, she hurried to the entrance.

Amusement brought a smile to his face as he watched her jog. Her blonde hair spread in a silken curtain behind her, glowing in the midday sun. Her skinny jeans brought out her long legs as she ran to the entrance. Everything she did was cute in a sexy way.

With a wistful sigh, he brought out his concert notes and memorized his first speech. Unfortunately, Carly wasn't the only one that had to perform. She was the professional, whereas he was just a poser, a vineyard-worker in disguise. He'd have to rely on the charm his friends teased him about. Hopefully it was enough to get him through. Reciting the phrases in Italian, then English, he walked to the entrance.

The black-costumed orchestra contrasted with the cream stone, showing life and vitality where only ghosts roamed. Maestro Braun was a wise man to choose such a location for the start of their tour. Carly gave the tuning note, and the entire string section surged with sound. The high rafters reverberated the harmony in a gorgeous echo effect.

Already, audience members with blankets and folding chairs chose seats along the tourist walkway. They held water bottles and flipped through the program notes with interest. Hopefully no one there recognized him and wondered why the charming vineyard bachelor had suddenly changed careers.

Checking to make sure he'd tied his silver necktie straight, Michelangelo took his place at the mic. He started with Italian, then translated to English. 'Greetings my fellow Italians. I have a special treat for you today. This wonderful orchestra visits us from Easthampton, Massachusetts. They've traveled a long way to play for us, and they have a wonderful program planned, starting with a well-known work by an Italian composer.'

The audience applauded, and Michelangelo did what he did best; smiled and looked good. His friends had always teased him about posing for wine commercials, but he'd only ever had eyes for working in the vineyard. Those grapevines were his home.

A home I will fight to keep.

Michelangelo introduced Ms. Maxhammer and Maestro Braun, showering them with every compliment he could think of.

The conductor walked on stage, and the orchestra stood in recognition. He clapped Michelangelo in a half-hug, and Michelangelo breathed with relief. He'd gotten through it without any real blunders. Taking a seat in the back next to the percussionists, Michelangelo searched the orchestra for Carly. If he tilted his head just right, he could see her profile as she brought her reed to her lips. As the music began, he listened for her every note.

*****

Carly had that same prickling sensation someone was watching her, and she had an idea who it was. Determined to focus on her measure-counting, she zeroed-in on her music and checked her reed. This time she'd sound like an oboe and less like a bird of prey.

Luscious chords began the opening measures to Gioachino Rossini's *Overture* to *The Barber of Seville*. Carly took a deep breath and came in with a long, anticipation-building note that rose into a glorious melody as the strings pulsed in accompaniment and a French horn saluted with arpeggios.

Carly echoed the strings before the chain of chords from the beginning returned. Then the strings introduced the main theme everyone knew so well from all of the Bugs Bunny cartoons. Goosebumps still prickled her arms as she played the tender and teasing oboe solo.

The music crescendoed to the grand finale of the piece, echoing over the stones. Despite the long flight and small amount of sleep, the orchestra sounded amazing. Applause erupted and Carly stood with the rest of the orchestra, basking in the glow of a perfect performance. Too bad her reprieve was short-lived. That ridiculous aria loomed after the intermission like a bad dream. Even after rehearsing all night, Alaina's tempo wasn't sitting right.

After the applause, Carly booked it off stage. The next piece had strings only, and she needed to get to the changing rooms and squeeze herself into Alaina's gaudy excuse for a concert gown.

The changing rooms, of course, were a makeshift tent by the bus near a Porta Potty. Edda came out of the bus drinking a bottle of water. With her short, curly dark hair and thick glasses, she looked like a sweet, little mom. 'Can I help you, signorina?'

Carly scanned the area for Michelangelo, but he must have been announcing the intermission. 'Yeah, I need my garment bag and a place to change.'

'Of course. One moment.' Edda disappeared into the bus and reappeared with the bag. Only one dress was left, meaning Alaina had already gotten the better one of the two. *Not that I'd fit into hers anyway.* With all of Alaina's curves, that dress would look like a disco ball on her. Besides, she didn't need the extra sparkles. All she needed to do was play her best. Who cared if she didn't look half as beautiful?

With Michelangelo out there, Carly hated to admit that *she* just might.

'Thank you.' Carly took the bag and slipped into the tent.

Alaina held up her hand mirror, applying a generous glob of red lipstick. Her red hair curled in waves down her bare back and her dress glittered like a Christmas ornament. 'Cutting it close, aren't you? Don't we go on in a few?'

'I had to play in the first piece.' Carly slipped off her black skirt. She wished she'd at least tried the dress on before they left. Changing five minutes before show time was more than risky.

She unzipped the bag and held the dress in front of her, trying to decide whether to pull it over her head or step into it.

Alaina snapped her mirror closed, looking at her as though she was a child who couldn't tie their shoes. 'Here, I'll help.'

The opera diva took the dress, scrunched it up like a slinky, and held it on top of Carly's head. 'Hold up your arms.'

Carly did as told, exhaling all of her breath just in case she needed that little extra space to slip it on. Alaina pulled the dress over her head and down to her feet. The material felt cool and slick against her body, shimmering with her every move.

Alaina's face fell, and her red lips pouted. 'Oh my.'

Anxiety raced all over Carly along with the light playing off the sparkles. *Oh no, the dress must look hideous. That, or I have a boob falling out.*

Carly glanced down, expecting the fit to horrify her. The fabric clung to her shape in all the right places, highlighting the curve of her breasts with a slight swell around her hips. A shade darker than Alaina's, the fabric had a dark sensuality to it that the diva's bright dress lacked.

She glanced back up at Alaina. 'What's the matter?'

Alaina stared at her with an icy glare. 'You look gorgeous. Better than me.'

She was right, but Carly didn't want to shove it in her face. 'I don't know about that. Your dress is…brighter.'

'Come on.' Alaina took her arm. 'We don't have time to fix it now.'

Like Carly would want to fix it? Sure, Alaina was the real star, but just because she'd chosen a glittery bomb didn't mean Carly couldn't look fabulous.

They walked in silence to the archway on stage left. Michelangelo stood at the microphone, speaking in Italian. After a pause, he switched to English.

'The next piece is an aria taken from a cantata which was commissioned to celebrate a wedding around seventeen hundred and eighteen. Titled, *Give way now, dismal shadows*, it speaks of cold winter transforming to spring and celebrates the dawning of new life and love.'

Or the dawning of embarrassment. Carly shifted back and forth, wanting to get the silly aria over with as soon as possible. Cocooned in her dress as she played, she felt like an oversized ballerina in a tutu that clung too tightly.

Michelangelo gestured toward them, 'May I introduce the lovely, talented ladies, Alaina Amaldi and Carly Davis.'

Lovely? Carly flushed as she followed Alaina on stage in front of the orchestra. *He's supposed to say that. It's his job, you idiot.*

Michelangelo's gaze swept past Alaina and settled on her. His eyes widened in shocked surprise, making her ultra-aware of the bare skin above her low-cut dress. He clasped hands with Alaina, wishing her well, then turned to Carly.

Carly reached her hand out, but Michelangelo ignored it,

leaning forward to kiss her on the cheek. He lingered for a long heartbeat and whispered in her ear, 'You look radiant.'

Feeling his breath on her cheek, Carly blushed and a tremble flowed through her. Turning to the audience, she felt like an ameba under the microscope. All eyes stared at her and her Italian love affair—which was never going to happen. *Focus on your music, you fool.*

Michelangelo exited the stage, leaving her with Alaina. The diva raised an eyebrow in a threat. The piece started with the oboe interlude. It was up to Carly to set the tone.

She checked her reed as Wolf glanced at her in anticipation. Silence reigned, and the Coliseum brimmed with expectation.

I can do this. We've only played it a hundred times. Carly nodded and breathed in, cueing the first note.

Eighth and sixteenth notes chirped from her oboe in a cheerful opening as the orchestra accompanied her. She pushed the tempo to fit Alaina's request, feeling as though she was running through a garden instead of leisurely strolling, kicking up sods of earth along the way.

Alaina came in with a bellow of vibrato. What should have been a carefree jaunt sounded more like a deluge of ostentation and glitter. Carly fought to keep up with the soprano's odd indulgences, holding some notes out, while pushing through others. Alaina was trying too hard, resulting in a gaudy jumble of words and notes.

The aria ended with a simple cadence, putting the music out of its misery. Carly allowed a moment of silence, then released her reed from her lips. Light applause trickled through the Coliseum. Most of the spectators wouldn't have any idea, but the ones that counted—Alaina's newspaper reviewers—would surely tear it apart.

Carly had done the exact opposite of what she wanted: she'd looked amazing, but played like a hot mess. *What have I done?*

CHAPTER SEVEN

Favor

Michelangelo checked the last row of bus seats, making sure no one had left anything important behind. He'd found a few half-used water bottles, an umbrella, and a concert program. Stuffing the program into his shirt, he thought back to Carly's duet with Alaina. She looked absolutely gorgeous in her burgundy dress, outshining the opera diva in every way.

His chest panged when he remembered her disappointed grimace as she walked off stage. He wasn't classically trained, and the aria sounded pleasant to him despite Alaina's earsplitting high notes. But something had gone wrong. Should he drop by Carly's room and reassure her? It was his job to ensure the comfort of everyone in the orchestra.

'Daydreaming, signore?' Edda turned from her steering wheel. She still had to fill the bus with gas for their excursion to St. Peter's Basilica and the drive to Florence in two days and was fretting about the time.

Michelangelo realized he was standing in the aisle with his arms full of trash. He smiled as though she'd caught him red-handed. 'Something like that.'

Edda gave him a motherly smile. 'She's a lucky girl, whoever she is.'

He dumped the trash in a bag at the front of the bus. 'How do you know I'm dreaming about a signorina?'

'A young man your age needs a little love in his life.' She glanced at his bare ring finger. 'I'm surprised you've gone on this long without it.'

For a moment, he almost told her about his vineyard, and how he didn't have the time for love. But, he couldn't implicate her in his forgery. Best she did her job, and he his.

Michelangelo smiled. 'Maybe now's the time, eh?' He said it as more of a joke to get her off his case. But, as the thought passed his mind, it left a lasting impression.

'See you tomorrow. Enjoy your night off.'

She nodded. 'Oh, I will. Got my grandson coming over. The child runs like a demon, destroying everything in his path.'

He gave her a look of horror and she chuckled. 'I wouldn't want to be anywhere else. Any plans for you?'

He really needed to return to his vineyard, but his contract had him attending the orchestra's needs twenty-four seven—which was the reason for the big check at the end. 'Not for me.'

'Who knows, something may pop up.' Edda must have sensed the wistfulness in his voice.

Yeah, like two hundred thousand euros? That was about the only thing that could make him happy. Well, that and spending more time with Carly. If he could make her feel better about her performance, then he'd done his job for the day. 'Thanks, Edda.'

Michelangelo walked off the bus and toward the hotel. Three fifty-two. Carly's room number. All he had to do was take the elevator up and stop by. He could use some excuse like checking the departure time for tomorrow's tour of the Vatican. They had been late to the bus this morning, so a short visit wouldn't seem too strange.

He entered the hotel, making a beeline for the elevators before he changed his mind. *One compliment about her performance, that's all.* He didn't know why, but he had a deep urge to comfort her.

What if Alaina is there as well?

Then he'd reaffirm the time with both of them, give Carly his reassurance about her performance and return to his room. What was the worst that could happen?

Michelangelo stepped into the elevator and pressed for the third floor. When he got out, the hallway was empty. *Grazie a Dio.* The less people who saw him here the better.

He counted the room numbers until he found three fifty-two. Excitement rushed through him. Brushing lint off the green polo he'd put on after the concert, he knocked on the door.

The door swung open, and Alaina leant on the wall, wearing black, lacy, sheer sleepwear—or underwear—he wasn't sure. 'Well, hello Michelangelo.' She stepped forward and he averted his eyes from all of the porcelain flesh. 'What can I do for you?'

He looked over her shoulder, but the room seemed empty. He cleared his throat, assuming the most professional tone he could under such circumstances. 'I wanted to reaffirm the time for the tour tomorrow.'

'Reaffirm away.' She trailed her long-nailed finger up and down the side of the door.

'The bus leaves at nine a.m. sharp. Can you make sure Carly receives my message?'

Alaina waved her finger in the air. 'Of course.'

'Good.' He moved to leave, and her hand darted at him like a viper, grabbing his arm. 'You can't fool me. I know why you're here.'

His heart sped into high gear. 'Excuse me?' Did she know about his attraction to Carly? He hadn't exactly done his best to hide it.

'Come in and I'll show you.'

Or worse: did she have some sort of evidence about his tour guide history—or lack thereof? Was she going to blackmail him? He only had about ten euros left to his name.

Michelangelo stepped in. 'My apologies, signorina. I have no idea what you are referring to.'

'This.'

Before he could take a breath, Alaina pushed herself against him, pressing her sticky, lipstick-coated mouth to his.

*****

If bombing the aria wasn't enough, Carly had another message from Dino on her phone. As everyone else shuffled upstairs, she found a quiet reception room and called her voicemail. Crossing her fingers, she hoped he wasn't dropping her as a performer.

Dino's voice came on the line. 'Carly. Babe. Boy, do I have a gig for you this Friday night.'

Carly breathed with relief, then rolled her eyes as the word *Friday* sank in. Didn't he hear her the first time? She was four thousand miles from Boston. That was quite some mileage to pay. She prepared to be majorly disappointed.

'It's at the—' He paused as if he either forgot the name or couldn't pronounce it. 'Cesari Amento, located right in the center of Rome.'

Wait a sec. Did he say Rome?

Carly ended the message and pressed speed dial.

'Dirty Dancing DJs.'

'Dino. It's Carly.'

'I knew you'd be a-callin'' Dino sounded like he was grinning at the same time as he spoke.

'How did you—'

'I pulled some strings. A former DJ of mine opened a business in Milan. He books all of Italy, and I thought—why not. Let's give it a try.'

'That's wonderful. The orchestra is off that night. I'm totally free.' Did she sound too desperate? She didn't care.

'How much Italian do you speak?'

Carly froze. *Never say no to a gig if you can help it.* 'Some.'

Meaning *Si* and *Grazie*. Oh, and *signore*. Put them together and she could say *Yes, thank you, Mr*. At least that's what she thought.

'Great. I'll hook you up. Their oboist dropped out last minute—hand problems or something. Anyways, the contact name is Vinci Romano, the lead violinist in the chamber group, and the booker is Mario Gallo.'

'Mario, as in the video game?'

'Yes, as in the video game. But, don't tell him that.'

Carly laughed. 'Don't worry. My lips are sealed.'

Dino typed in the background. 'I'm sending you the times and address in an e-mail.'

Address. Carly hadn't thought about how she'd get there. *Guess I'll have to call a cab.*

'Thanks, Dino. I owe you one.'

'No, I owe you. Expanding my business overseas is a dream I've had for a long time.'

Wow, getting on Dino's good side was a score. 'I'll make sure to do a good job, then.'

'You always do, babe.'

She ended the conversation and hung up. *Looks like the day is shaping up after all.* She only had to gloss over one little detail. She couldn't speak Italian to save her life.

Carly needed an Italian teacher, like, yesterday, and only one person came to mind.

Michelangelo.

Drat. Hadn't she vowed to stay away from him? Could she really control herself if he hit on her again?

She'd have to chance it. Gathering her oboe case and purse, Carly approached the front desk and asked for Michelangelo's room number, saying she had some sort of problem with the tour to resolve. They gave it to her right away.

Carly stepped in the elevator and pressed his floor. Waiting for the door to open, she rehearsed what she'd say. *Please teach me Italian in twenty-four hours.* Every excuse she came up with sounded crazy, so she decided to stick with the truth.

The elevator dinged and the doors opened. She stepped out and followed the numbers to his room at the end of the hall.

I can't believe I'm doing this. Sheepishly, she smoothed down her black blouse and knocked on the door.

No answer.

Maybe he was an early sleeper.

She pushed away yet another image of Michelangelo in his boxer shorts and knocked again.

Nothing.

He must be helping someone else resolve an issue about the tour.

Dammit. She needed him now. How could she learn anything tomorrow in St. Peter's Basilica while he regaled the orchestra with historical facts?

Carly thought about walking around to look for him, but that bordered on stalker behavior, and she didn't want to advertise the fact she was seeking him out in the wee hours of the night, even though it was purely work-related.

Carly brought out her purse and wrote on the back of a grocery receipt. *Need your help with Italian translation asap. Carly Davis, Room three fifty-two.* There. That sounded professional.

She slipped the paper under the door. Now she could go back to her room and look up key phrases on her phone and start memorizing right away. Michelangelo could help with pronunciation.

Carly took the elevator back to her room. Disappointment settled over her and she tried to push away her illogical feelings. Was it because he couldn't help her right away? Or was she really so hung up over a tour guide she'd barely met? If it was the latter, then she had to slap some sense into herself. She needed him for her gig and that was it. End of story. No flirting allowed.

The door to her and Alaina's room stood ajar, with golden light glowing into the hallway. Panic jolted through her. Alaina would never leave the door open with all of her expensive jewelry and perfume. Had someone broken in?

A thud reverberated from inside. Was it luggage hitting the floor, or a body hitting the wall? What if the intruders were attacking Alaina?

She reached for her phone to call nine-one-one. Then she remembered they were in Italy, and she had no idea who to call. By the time she figured it out, Alaina would be dead.

Carly held her purse as a weapon and her oboe case as a shield. She whirled around the corner into the room.

Alaina leaned against the wall, kissing a man. She wore see-through undies, which didn't leave much to the imagination.

Carly blushed with embarrassment and looked away immediately. 'Holy Mary, mother of Victoria's Secret! Sorry to intrude.'

Alaina pulled back, and Carly's stomach dropped to ground level.

'Michelangelo?' What a hopeless flirt. Had he seduced every naïve woman on that tour bus? She felt so utterly stupid.

'My apologies.' He looked more shocked than she was. *Didn't think both women you hit on had the same room, you jerk?*

Carly glanced back to Alaina, who leaned against the wall with a self-satisfied smirk. 'We were just discussing the departure time for the tour tomorrow.'

'I'm sure.' Carly turned back toward the door. 'I can find somewhere else to sleep if you two want to be alone.' There was no way the three of them would be having a slumber party.

Michelangelo pushed by both of them. 'No, there's no need. I was just leaving.' He glanced at Carly one more time, his eyes looking innocently vulnerable considering the circumstances. 'I'm sorry, Ms. Davis.'

Carly gawked with nothing to say as he left. A second after he was gone, she thought of all the wittiest responses in the world.

'You scared him away.' Alaina pouted. 'We were having such a good time.'

'You could have let me know so I didn't walk into the most awkward moment of my life.'

'It was a surprise, dear. After the embarrassment of our aria, I needed something to cheer me up.'

Carly sighed, still reeling from the second embarrassment of the day. 'And I didn't?'

'Wait a sec.' Alaina crossed the room and narrowed her eyes at Carly. 'Are you jealous?'

'Hardly.' Carly picked up her phone as an excuse not to meet her gaze. She didn't want to see so much of Alaina's skin anyway.

Alaina put both hands on her hips. 'How do I know you don't want him for yourself?'

Carly collapsed on the bed wondering if she could learn Italian from Wikipedia and Google. She had a gig to prepare for. The last thing she needed was idle distractions. *What a total waste of thought and time.*

'Believe me, I don't.' She gave Alaina a thumbs-up. 'He's all yours.'

CHAPTER EIGHT

Details

'So the Pope and a lawyer reach the gate to heaven.' Al leaned over expectantly at Carly as Edda drove the tour bus toward St. Peter's Square. Still ruffled by the memory of a mostly naked Alaina and her red lipstick smudged on Michelangelo's lips, Carly didn't have the willpower to fight him off.

'And?' She hoped this wasn't a dirty joke.

Al grinned. 'So, all these saints, angels, and other holy people flock around the lawyer. They carry him on their shoulders and cheer. The Pope doesn't get the time of day.'

Carly bit her lip. *I have no idea where this is going, but it can't be good.* 'Go on.'

A few of the violinists turned around in their seats with eyebrows raised. Al nodded to them and raised his voice. 'So the Pope is pretty disappointed—I mean, I'd be disappointed—working for God my whole life just to be short-changed in the end. That's like me meeting some Low Brass God and having him show more interest in a piccolo player! Anyways, St. Peter comes down and tells him not to worry.'

'Why?' Carly felt as though she was walking into a trap, but anything was better than thinking about Alaina's black lingerie.

'St. Peter explains they get popes in there all the time, but it's not every day they get a lawyer!' He slapped his knee. 'Ba dum dum.'

'Hearty har har.' Carly shook her head but smiled despite herself. The older violin ladies chuckled.

Mike, Al's brass buddy and suspected drinking partner clapped from the front of the bus. 'Tell us another one, Al.'

'Don't encourage him,' Carly shouted. Her eyes scanned the bus, landing on Michelangelo. Dark circles edged his gorgeous eyes as he sat next to Alaina Chatterbox. He gave Carly a longing, melancholy look, as if they were lovers having a quarrel. She flicked her eyes up in annoyance and turned to the windows.

The dome of the basilica stood in the center, surrounded by a semicircle of thick columns on either side. Within stood an obelisk, like a giant sundial. The grand scale dwarfed all of the tourists in the square. Even if Carly had brought her camera, she wouldn't have been able to capture the full effect in one complete shot.

'It's amazing,' she whispered under her breath to no one in particular.

Michelangelo's voice boomed on the intercom. 'Welcome to St. Peter's Basilica, a late Renaissance church designed by…', he glanced down at his hand, 'Donato Bramante, Carlo Maderno, and Gian Lorenzo Bernini and, of course, Michelangelo—not meaning myself, by the way.'

While a few members of the orchestra chuckled, Alaina let out the biggest laugh Carly had ever heard. *Must be those opera-singer lungs.*

Michelangelo cleared his throat and adjusted his collar, as if the heat had risen on the bus. 'St. Peter's is the most renowned work of Renaissance architecture and one of the largest churches in the world.' He shut off the intercom.

Carly thought he'd go into more detail. It was arguably the most famous place in all of Italy, and maybe even in the world.

That's odd. She kind of wanted to know more about it, not

having had the time to look it up back in Boston. *Maybe he'd say more during the tour.*

As she got off the bus, she made sure not to look into Michelangelo's eyes. They'd had enough awkward moments, and she bet every time he looked at her he thought of how she'd interrupted his kiss with Alaina. Not the most favorable memory to keep dredging up. Thankfully, Bertha needed extra help getting her purse from the overhead, so he was too busy to notice Carly sneaking by.

The Italian summer air warmed Carly in a bath of sunlight as she walked across the square. A sudden urge to spread her arms and whirl around amidst all of the majesty overcame her, reminding her there was more to life than orchestra seats and gigs. The sheer size stole her breath away, making her feel like a speck in the middle of a giant universe.

Someone grabbed Carly's arm and she whirled around. 'Got another joke for me, Al?'

Michelangelo stood beside her. At the mention of Al's name he shifted uncomfortably. 'I need to speak with you.' In his hands he held a small receipt.

The note! She'd forgotten all about it. 'Oh that. Never mind, I've found another teacher.' Yeah, Google and Speak Italian dot com.

Michelangelo scratched his brow as if what he was about to say was difficult. 'First of all, I'm sorry about last night.'

Great. The one subject she didn't want to talk about. Carly waved him off. 'You can kiss whomever you want. Why should I care? I should be apologizing for interrupting.'

She walked toward the fountain in the middle of the square, and he followed her, wincing at her words. 'It was never my intention to kiss Alaina.'

'Already told you—none of my business. Go ahead and date who you want.' Carly opened her phone to pretend to take a picture, but he grabbed her arm.

'Why do you need an Italian translator?'

She wiggled out of his grip. 'No reason. Just curious. That's all.'

'Your note made it sound fairly important.'

Carly fumbled with the camera function on her phone. She was always too busy to use it, so she had no idea how to quickly snap a picture. 'I'm a little overly dramatic at times.'

She swallowed down her lie like a rock in her throat. That didn't sound like her at all. Where was Al and his pope jokes when she needed him? Turning to the fountain, she hoped Michelangelo would just go away.

'I hope you're not planning on sneaking off during your stay.' His voice dropped to a velvety low, suspicious tone, and Carly held her breath.

What? Was he now their chaperone as well? She turned back toward him and narrowed her eyes. 'Don't you have a tour to be giving?'

'I'm just warning you, not everyone speaks English, and if you don't know the city, you could end up in a shady part of town. I can't have something bad happen on one of *my* tours.'

'I can assure you I can take care of myself. Just because I'm a classical oboist doesn't mean I'm not a ninja in disguise.'

Self-satisfied with her clever retort, Carly turned to walk away.

Michelangelo grabbed her arm. He leaned toward her, and his voice fell to a whisper. 'Either I assign a luggage boy to watch your room and stop you from sneaking off, or I help you with what you need and turn my back. Either way, your choice.'

Carly froze. Could she trust him not to tell Ms. Maxhammer? No. She couldn't even trust him to keep his lips in his own hotel room.

A playful sparkle returned to his eyes. 'What if you ask where the concert is and someone says *Vada dritto! E poi giri a destra.*'

He spoke so fast, it all sounded like one big slurred word. 'Huh?'

He crossed his arms. 'My point exactly.'

Carly fidgeted with her purse strap. Maybe he chose a really strange saying just to prove his point. 'So what does it mean?'

'Go straight, then turn right.'

'Oh.'

Michelangelo teased her with a raised eyebrow. She had to admit he looked good in his navy button-down shirt and easy-going jeans that hung in just the right places. 'Or what if they ask *come si chiama?*'

She put her hands on her hips. Two could play this game. She'd learned a few things last night on her phone. '*Non sono affari tuoi!*'

He grinned. 'Your *name* is none of my business?'

Whoops. Carly's face fell. 'I thought you were asking where I lived.'

He tossed his head back, his luscious waves of hair falling around his shoulders. 'There's no hope.'

What if Michelangelo was right? She didn't want to make a fool of herself at one of Dino's gigs—his first gig in Italy. He trusted her to do a good job, and how could she do her best if she had no idea what they were saying? She might even piss someone off in the process.

She sighed. 'Fine. It's a gig at the Cesari Amento, tomorrow night at 7 p.m. I need to learn as much Italian as I can between now and then.'

His beautiful eyes widened. 'Tomorrow night?'

'Can you help me or not?'

Michelangelo pursed his lips as if considering. 'I can. Meet me for lunch around noon at Caffè Picasso on Via Crescenzio.'

He turned to leave and she grabbed *his* arm. 'Why can't we start right now?'

The side of his lips curled as he gestured toward the square. 'Like you said, signorina, I have a tour to give.'

*****

Michelangelo rounded up all of the orchestra members with a boundless sense of relief. He'd tossed and turned all night, trying to figure out a way to get Carly to forgive him. Even though his logical mind told him he'd never see her again after two weeks, he couldn't have her thinking he was some Italian womanizer romancing all the young ladies on his tours.

Not only had he seemingly led her on with his flirting, but then she'd found him with her roommate on the same night she'd been devastated by her performance in the solo. What kind of an awful tour guide does that?

He had to make it up to her, and helping her learn Italian for her gig was the ideal way. This was beyond what Ms. Maxhammer had said about making sure each orchestra member was comfortable. This was about reinstating his honor.

Michelangelo led the orchestra to the steps of the basilica and into the grand cathedral. Thinking about Carly had kept his mind off his tour job, and he'd left most of his notecards back at the hotel. He had no idea what he was going to say.

Every one of them stared wide-eyed, awed by the ornate artistry and high ceilings. Even Michelangelo felt a sense of reverent peace, stealing his breath away as he passed through the high arches. He hadn't visited since a field trip in upper secondary school. Since the last time he went, the church had seemed to grow vaster.

Michelangelo brought the group to a quiet alcove and thought back to what he'd learned in *università*.

'Welcome to St. Peter's Basilica. Legend has it St. Peter, one of the twelve apostles of Jesus, was buried right below the altar.'

Darin, the son of one of the violinists, raised his hand. He did the whole Gothic rocker look, with two earrings in his upper ear. 'When was this built?'

Ummmm, a long time ago. Michelangelo thought back to his studies. 'There has been a church at this site since the fourth century.'

'Yeah, dude, but when was *this* place built?' His blue-haired sister, Trixie, didn't even bother to raise her hand. Crossing her arms over her emo band t-shirt, she chewed a big wad of gum and blew a bubble. An iPod ear bud hung from one ear.

Impetuous, rude Americans.

He considered ignoring the question, but Ms. Maxhammer looked on with interest.

Michelangelo scratched his head. Who kept track of these things? 'In the Renaissance, of course. Fifteen hundred and… twenty…six-ish.' His voice trailed off and he coughed. *Smoother than gelato, right.* If only his friends could see him now. Pandering to Americans just to buy one more month's rent.

All eyes stayed on him, so he waved his arm at the ceiling. The place could speak for itself. 'You can see the Renaissance architecture is typical of that time. Go ahead, take a walk around and see for yourself.'

The group dispersed and he sighed with relief.

A woman in her forties approached him. She wore a blouse buttoned right to the top, with her dark hair pulled back into a severe ponytail. He might have seen her playing the cello somewhere in the back but he couldn't exactly remember because his eyes had been focused on Carly. 'Can I help you?'

'You said this cathedral was built in the fifteen hundred and twenties, but I distinctly remember learning in a documentary on the History Channel they started building in April of fifteen hundred and six.' She challenged him with a haughty glare in her eyes.

Rude American number two. Somehow, he wasn't surprised.

Michelangelo crossed his arms and leaned back on his heels. 'Yes, well, some speculate the original architects began even before that, in fifteen hundred and three in a secret society, in the original underground church. They called themselves…the Manifesto.'

Her eyes widened, and he resisted the urge to smile. 'The Brotherhood of the Manifesto claimed St. Peter whispered to them himself in spirit form—giving them the dimensions to represent a cruciform shape. Tell that to the History Channel.'

She adjusted her skinny, rimmed glasses. 'They said nothing

about it.'

He held up a finger like he'd checkmated them in a chess game. 'Nor would they.' He raised an eyebrow. 'Because it's secret.' *Argue that.*

She opened her mouth, but he silenced her with a finger. 'Excuse me. I have to check on the others outside.'

Michelangelo exited the Basilica and breathed in the fresh air. He collapsed on the first step. *How am I ever going to get through the day?* He dug out his phone and did a Google search on the Basilica. The cellist had been correct. They did start to build in fifteen hundred and six then finished in sixteen twenty six. Why couldn't he remember?

Because you thought you'd ruined your chances with Carly. That's why.

Michelangelo rubbed his temples. He had to focus on what was really important; doing a great job to get the paycheck that would buy his vineyard and everyone who lived and worked on it more time. Everything else was secondary. As much as he wanted to make things right with Carly, he had to make sure he was still performing at his best.

He brought up the Wikipedia article on the Basilica, and started memorizing all the facts.

One of four Papal Basilicas or Major Basilicas of Rome.

The church covers an area of two point three hectares, or five point seven acres.

A scream interrupted his thoughts.

Michelangelo glanced up from his phone.

Bertha and Trudy stood at the bottom of the steps. Bertha pointed to a skinny man in a torn black leather coat running between the columns with a woman's white purse. 'Thief!'

Anger welled up inside him as he threw himself down the stairs. Sweet little old Bertha, who'd told him to call her Bert and said he'd be a treat for the ladies had been victimized. Hadn't he heard her husband had passed away? What if she had an irreplaceable picture of him in her purse?

He launched after the thief, pushing through the crowd. Years of hauling barrels up and down the hills of his vineyard had given him well-developed muscles in his legs. If he could do one thing, he could run.

The thief bolted in between the columns, trying to lose him in the shadows. Michelangelo cut across the square, predicting the thief would head for the streets. He was small, maybe only a teenager, with oily brown hair stuck to the side of his head. *A little young for a criminal mastermind.* A pang of guilt passed through Michelangelo's gut before he remembered this teenage hoodlum had stolen sweet little old Bertha's purse.

Michelangelo closed in, reaching out for the coat just as the boy zigzagged into the oncoming traffic. His fingernails grazed the leather as the boy ducked and rolled between tires.

Michelangelo winced as drivers honked and veered to avoid hitting him. The boy stood and threw himself across the hood of a car.

Michelangelo rounded the bumper and reached out as the boy rolled back onto his feet. His fingers closed on thin air. *Merda!*

The boy dashed into the alley on the other side of the street. Michelangelo raised his hands against the beeping cars and followed.

The alley reeked of old trash and decay. Michelangelo stumbled over a crumpled cardboard box. A brick wall blocked the end of the alley, so either the boy was hiding, or he'd found an unlocked back door.

In this city, everyone locked their doors.

'You're cornered, son. Come on out and give back the purse, and I won't press charges.' Michelangelo's voice reverberated on the high brick walls. He passed a dumpster and lifted the lid. Bags of trash and old food sat in heaps inside. The smell choked him and he dropped the lid.

Before Michelangelo could react, a fist came out of nowhere, hitting him square in the jaw. He stumbled backward, losing his balance as the boy jumped over him.

Nimble little stinker.

Reaching up, Michelangelo grabbed the boy's rolled-up jeans cuff and yanked him down. The boy fell beside him on his stomach.

He scrambled up, but Michelangelo moved quickly, pinning him with both his arms. The purse was strapped to the boy's shoulder. He'd have to let go of one hand to get it off.

The boy spat in his face, muttering profanities.

Michelangelo blinked as he saw the broken nose, chipped front tooth and freckled face.

So much like…

He loosened his grip and swung off the purse before the boy could fight back. He had what he came for. But, he didn't let go.

'You gonna turn me in?' The boy's eyes narrowed in a mean glare, but underneath, Michelangelo could see the desperation and the pain.

'No. I want you to get out there, find a job, and stop stealing. Do something with your life.'

The boy sneered. 'Why do you care?'

Of course. Just like him…

What could he do? Even if the boy promised him to stop stealing, he could go back on the streets and do it again tomorrow. Sixty-one million people lived in Italy. He'd never see Michelangelo again.

Instead, he let him up. With one hand he held onto the boy's shirt, and with the other Michelangelo dug out his wallet. The little street urchin squirmed in his grasp as he offered him a business card and his last ten euros. 'Here. You want a real job? Tell Isabella that Michelangelo sent you. Now, go get yourself something to eat.'

The boy with the freckled face gave him a suspicious glare but swiped the bill and the card. In ten seconds he'd disappeared back into the street.

Michelangelo stood and brushed off his pants. His jaw ached, and he rubbed his chin. The little bugger had a pretty strong left hook. Michelangelo hoped he had proven to the boy that some-body did care.

Emerging back on the bustling streets, Michelangelo clutched Bertha's purse to his side in a death grip just in case someone else got the same idea. He scanned the streets, but there was no sign of the boy. As he walked across the street, he brought out his phone.

'Ricci Vineyards, how may I help you?'

'Hey Isabella. How are things?'

She sighed. 'The same as always. We managed to sell thirty crates yesterday, which will keep us going for another week. But our stock is low.'

'I know. Last year's drought really took a toll on production. Just hang in there. This crop will be the best yield yet.'

'I hope so.' She sounded wistful, like she didn't believe him.

'Hey, Isabella?'

'Si?'

'If a scraggly boy with freckles and a chipped tooth comes in looking for work, just put him out in the fields and pay him like the others, okay?' It was a long shot, but he'd told the boy to go, and he was going to keep his word.

'Still picking up strays, huh?' Amusement tinged her voice.

'Yeah.' Sure, some of them would find their way back to the streets, but even if he saved one, then it was worth it. If only he had the euros to offer more jobs.

'You're a kind-hearted man, and good things will come.'

'Let's hope so.' Michelangelo sighed, wishing Carly could see him the same way.

He ended his conversation with Isabella and walked across the square. The entire orchestra had collected on the steps to the Basilica, sitting in rows just like they did in concert.

'There he is!' One of the violists shouted, pointing across the square.

Michelangelo waved. Had they all been waiting for him?

Bertha stood and shouted. 'My purse! He found my purse.'

Everyone cheered and clapped, and some people chanted his name. Ms. Maxhammer stood off to the side, giving him a nod of approval. He hadn't done it for her. He'd done it for Bertha.

Michelangelo never blushed, but slight warmth burned in his cheeks. He gave Bertha her purse back, and she hugged it to her chest. 'Thank you, hon.'

'Not a problem, signora.'

Her friend, Trudy, narrowed her eyes. 'Did you catch the thief?'

Michelangelo glanced away, still thinking of the poor boy's chipped tooth. 'No, he got away.'

CHAPTER NINE

The Best of the Best

Carly couldn't believe her eyes. The same man she'd seen romancing Alaina right after hitting on her had run across the square for Bertha's purse like a bona fide hero.

Boy, he must have wanted to impress Ms. Maxhammer, or Alaina, or herself—*or all three of us*. There was no other possible motivation. She couldn't believe someone that self-centered would ever put himself out like that. Not only did he look as though he'd crawled through the dump, but the right side of his face was red and bruised. *That* would hurt in the morning.

Still, she needed him. Carly checked her watch. Eleven thirty. She should start walking to the café now so no one saw them walk off in the same direction. Ducking out behind the orchestra's cheers, she made her way across the square.

She walked until she found a painted sign swinging on a lamp post with warped letters that read *Caffè Picasso*. Yellow and green striped awnings spread over window boxes of bluebells and violets. Cast-iron chairs and small round tables covered with bright umbrellas sprawled into the street. A woman sipped a latte with a little fluffy white dog that barked as Carly entered.

A tiny bell tinkled as she closed the door behind her. Carly stared at the chalkboard full of Italian writing in all colors of the rainbow. The attendant behind the register glanced up with a smile. '*Posso aiutarla?*'

'Um…' Carly thought back to her studies last night. '*Lei parla inglese?*'

'Si. What can I get for you?' The cashier smiled and Carly breathed with relief. Thank goodness Michelangelo had agreed to help. She couldn't even figure out how to order with the translation apps on her phone.

After ordering a pastrami panini and a chai latte, Carly settled into a seat inside the café at a booth. Even though she'd love to enjoy the nice summer weather and watch the passersby, she didn't want Alaina, or anyone else from the orchestra, spotting her alone with Michelangelo.

Even though her logical mind warned her she was playing with fire, struggling to understand that chalkboard had confirmed her need for his help.

A server came by with her food and drink.

'*Grazie.*' She took a sip, savoring the spicy taste on her tongue.

The bell tinkled, and Carly's heart sped. She peered around the booth.

Michelangelo met her gaze and gave her a heart-melting smile. He walked to the cashier, who gave him a long, wistful look up and down. Michelangelo placed his order in smooth, flowing Italian.

After paying with a credit card, he filed into the booth across from Carly. 'Enjoying your lunch?'

Her turkey sandwich had sat uneaten. When her nerves acted up, she was never hungry. 'The latte is delicious.'

'Too bad.' He pouted his gorgeous, kissable lips. 'I ordered a tea.'

'I'm sure that's good, too.'

The server came by with Michelangelo's food and drink. Giving him one last, longing look, she walked away.

'So, you've had an exciting day.' Carly addressed one of the elephants in the room. Even if he had done it to impress all the ladies, not mentioning his single act of heroism would make her look like the self-centered one.

'You could say that.' Michelangelo took a bite of his sandwich.

She resisted the urge to stroke his sore cheek. 'I hope you didn't hurt yourself too badly.'

'Naw. It was more careless than anything.' He sipped his tea.

'Too bad you didn't catch the lowlife responsible.' Carly tried a bite of her sandwich.

'I let him go.'

She almost choked on the wheat bread. 'You what?'

Michelangelo shrugged. 'He was just a boy, and he reminded me so much of someone from my childhood.' He shook his head, his eyes, which were amber-blue depths of compassion. 'I couldn't do it.'

Carly knew she had to get started on learning Italian, but he'd piqued her curiosity. 'Who did he remind you of?'

'Ricco Pinasco.' His eyes turned dark, like the ocean in a storm. 'My father found him hiding in one of the unused wine barrels on a cold, rainy night when I was a small boy. We were about the same age, although he was shorter than me.' He laughed. 'And tougher. My family took him in and he became a brother to me. We grew up together, playing in the grapevines, attending the local school. He was smarter than some of the teachers, but he couldn't seem to shake his past.'

Carly just stared, wondering why Michelangelo was telling her so much. She didn't interrupt him because she wanted to know more.

'He got into drugs and started stealing wine to sell on the streets. I pleaded with my father to give him another chance, but he threw Ricco out. I never saw him again.'

'I'm sorry.' Carly shook her head. She had a sister who'd become a teacher back in Massachusetts. Even though they didn't always see each other because of their busy schedules, she couldn't imagine losing her to some addiction.

'It's okay. It happened a long time ago.' Michelangelo glanced up at the ceiling. 'If he's not dead, then he's in a prison somewhere.'

'Have you tried to look for him?'

'Of course I have. Part of me is afraid of what I'll find, if he'll remember me, or if he does, if he'll hate me.'

'Sounds like you did all you could.'

Michelangelo leaned back. 'I wonder if I'd done something different, maybe he'd still be around. You know, visiting at the holidays, or working on the vineyard.'

'You can't change the past. All you can do is try to make a better future.'

Michelangelo pointed a finger at her as if she had the answer he wanted. 'That's what I intend to do. When I saw the boy with Bertha's purse, I wanted to end the cycle. I wanted to try to save him. So I gave him my card and some money and offered him a job at my vineyard.'

'You did?' Was this the same man who'd kissed Alaina? Was there such a thing as a compassionate, kind-hearted playboy? Something didn't add up, and Carly intended to get to the bottom of it.

Michelangelo sipped his tea, totally unaware of her microscopic observations of his character. 'Who knows if he'll ever show. But at least I tried my best.'

'And what if he does?' Carly leaned across the table. Would he really go through with it and hire him as a worker?

He winked, unconcerned. 'I'll have my secretary keep her eye on him. She's got a little boy of her own, so she knows how to keep them in line.'

Carly sipped her latte. *So, he's got a secretary. Must be quite some winery his family owns.*

Michelangelo finished his panini. 'So! *Cominciamo.*'

'What?' Carly didn't know if it was a question, a statement, or an offer. If the latter, she was *not* going to accept.

Michelangelo spread his hands out and smiled. 'Let's begin.'

'Okay.' Carly had no idea what he had in store for her, but she had to admit she was intrigued. 'What are you going to teach me first?'

His lips curled and she couldn't tell if it was a smile or a smirk. '*É un piacere conoscerla.*'

She shifted uncomfortably. 'What does it mean?'

'Say it.' He teased her with his eyes.

She crossed her arms over her chest. 'Not if you don't tell me what it means. I could be swearing profanities for all I know, or…professing my love.' Carly blushed. She wasn't about to admit to something she didn't—or did—feel. 'What kind of a teacher doesn't teach what the words mean?'

The kind who wants to flirt.

Michelangelo raised his hand. 'I'm only trying to start with the pronunciation first, and then the syntax. Do you want to learn or should I assign the luggage boy to watch your room?'

Okay, maybe he didn't want to flirt. She sighed, stifling a rebellious current of disappointment. 'What was it again?'

He repeated the phrase, the consonants and vowels slipping by her ear in a jumble.

'*Eh unnn piachay conosarla.*' Carly felt like her tongue was a brick in her mouth.

Michelangelo chuckled and covered his mouth with his hand.

Embarrassment crawled up her spine. It's not like language was her specialty. She wasn't a trained, bilingual tour guide. 'Hey, that's not fair. Let's put an oboe in your hands and see how you do.'

'Very badly, I would assume.' Michelangelo reached across the table and touched her hand. 'I'm sorry. I'll speak slower. Watch my lips.' He repeated the phrase.

Carly could watch his lips all day, but she wasn't there to flirt, she was there to learn Italian for her gig. She paid closer attention and repeated the phrase.

Michelangelo's eyes brightened. '*Eccellente!*' He took both her hands in his and squeezed.

Her heart raced as blood pumped into her cheeks. How could

one man have such a mind-numbing effect on her? She pulled away, wondering if this was such a good idea. Could she really trust him to teach her what she needed to learn for this gig or was she wasting her time? 'What did I just say?'

'Nice to meet you.' He placed his hands in his lap as if trying to restrain them. 'You're going to need to say something when you meet the other musicians, aren't you?'

'Yes, I am.' That was the perfect thing to learn. She said it again, committing it to memory. Thank goodness she had a knack for remembering sounds. 'Tell me more about common sayings.'

Michelangelo smiled and spouted another phrase. They went back and forth repeating sayings until the waitress came back with an annoyed look.

'Will there be anything else?' She'd cleared their plates a long time ago, so she just wiped off the countertop with a rag.

Michelangelo checked his watch. '*Mio dio*! We've been sitting here for almost two hours.'

Had it been that long? Time seemed to fly. Carly didn't want their conversation to end. She still had a lot to learn.

Michelangelo leaned over and whispered. 'Now's the chance to try your Italian.'

Carly shook her head. 'I don't know what you mean.'

He gave her a covert wink. 'Order one dessert. Tell her we'll share it.'

Sharing a dessert? Wasn't that a little too familiar? Carly balked. 'I don't know.'

He leaned back. 'Go on. I'll have anything you want.'

The waitress tapped her pen on her pad. 'Yes?'

Carly had better come up with something. They had already overstayed their welcome, and they really should order an additional item and leave a tip. If she didn't order anything else, they'd be expected to leave, and she had more Italian to learn.

'Okay.' She thought back to everything he'd gone over so far and gave it her best shot.

The waitress jotted something down on her pad and left. Carly turned to Michelangelo. 'Well?'

Michelangelo smiled and slipped into the booth beside her, picking up his fork. 'Looks like we'll be having some chocolate cake.'

*****

Michelangelo exited the café, wondering why he'd spoken so candidly to Carly. He'd given her way too much information about his vineyard, practically telling her he was the one in charge. Not only that, but he'd brought up his father. If she'd asked about him, then she'd know Michelangelo had inherited the vineyard only a few years ago and he wasn't in the tour business at all.

Mio Dio. What was I thinking?

After seeing how quickly Carly picked up Italian, he knew he was dealing with a clever mind, someone who could break down his façade with only a few more facts.

But for some reason, on top of all that, he'd volunteered to drive her to the gig.

Might as well demolish my vineyard right now.

Her sheer determination and vulnerability touched him, making him believe he could tell her anything. He'd have to watch his mouth around her, because who knew what she'd report back to Ms. Maxhammer if she learned the truth.

From his own personal experience, Americans were not to be trusted. They were all in it for their own good, and had no respect for things like vineyards, or ancient cathedrals, or tour guides.

But was Carly one of them?

Michelangelo turned back toward the café, where Carly still sat inside, looking over the notes he'd given her.

'Mr. Ricci! We meet again.'

He whirled around like someone caught looking in the windows of a women's underwear store. 'Alaina.'

The opera diva snaked her arm through his. 'I've been looking all around for you.' She glanced to the café. 'Just ate lunch?'

Oh no. This could be disastrous. If Carly decided to come out at that particular moment, Alaina would know they'd eaten together. She'd have a fit—she might even complain to Ms. Maxhammer he'd been philandering with the women in the orchestra.

'Yes. But I wouldn't recommend their food. Too stale.'

A woman sipping a latte overheard him and stared down at her drink.

Alaina raised both eyebrows. 'Is that so? I was just about to go in and get a coffee.'

'No, no, no.' He pulled her away from the door. 'You don't want to do that.'

She creased her painted eyebrows in confusion. 'What do you mean?'

'For you, may I present only the best of the best of Italy.' He clamped down on her grip of his arm. 'Let me show you the best place for coffee.'

'Well, then.' She smiled. 'Only you would know.'

Hoping Carly didn't see them leaving together, he directed Alaina as far out of sight as possible toward another café down the street. Ironically, the coffee at that one had a lighter brew. But, looking at the way Alaina stared into his eyes, he didn't think she'd notice.

CHAPTER TEN

Life Away

Carly hid her black clothes underneath a bright-pink scarf and floral blazer. The orchestra members were supposed to be having a night out on the town, and she didn't want anyone knowing she'd snuck off for another gig, with another orchestra, with Michelangelo.

She'd spent the day memorizing the notes she'd taken with Michelangelo yesterday at lunch and watching Italian television shows while the rest of the orchestra went on a tour of the local marketplace. He'd even called her room on his break, speaking Italian, to make sure she was absorbing the information. He'd given her an exact time when he'd pick her up in a red Fiat out front.

Alaina had gone shopping for a better dress, and knowing her, that would take all day. Thank goodness she hadn't come back yet. The less the opera diva knew, the better. She'd probably want to rehearse again, and Carly had had enough of Bach's silly rendition of love.

Making sure the hallway was clear, Carly snuck from her room and took the stairs down to the main lobby. Three floors weren't bad, but after walking all over the Vatican City, her feet ached.

Such is the price for a flourishing career.

Melody and Wolf sat on the guest sofas right before the double doors, chatting with Bertha, Trudy, and Al. At least one of them would notice her leaving all by herself. Then she'd have to come up with some excuse, not to mention the fact they might catch her getting in Michelangelo's car.

Great.

Carly closed the door and leaned against the wall in the stair shaft, trying to calm her racing heart. Maybe if she waited it out, they'd go away.

She checked her watch. Five more minutes and Michelangelo would pull up to the curb, expecting her to get in. She had to be at the Cesari Amento in thirty minutes, ready to play.

An older couple came down the stairs speaking feverishly in Italian, and Carly whipped out her phone, pretending to read an e-mail. As they passed, she picked up a few key phrases about hailing a taxi and eating out at some restaurant. The haze of foreign phrases had cleared some, thanks to Michelangelo.

The couple walked into the lobby and Carly checked again before the heavy fire door snapped shut.

Laughing, Wolf and Melody headed toward the entrance. Bertha and Trudy hailed an elevator, and Al leaned against the main desk, flirting with the dark-haired woman receptionist, who wasn't buying it.

Carly snuck out and hid behind a large ceramic pot almost as tall as her with exotic ferns splaying out on all sides. Her fingers brushed a picture of a young couple sitting beside a pond. Strangely, the woman and man had the same hair color as her light-blond ponytail and Michelangelo's dark waves. Blinking the resemblance away, she watched as Melody and Wolf disappeared outside.

Carly waited another two minutes and bolted for the door.

Sleek black limos, brightly colored taxis, and other luxury cars lined the circular drive. Melody and Wolf slipped into a taxi to

91

the right, so she turned left. *Come on, Michelangelo, where are you?*

A corner of red poked out from behind their tour bus to her left. Carly dashed down the sidewalk and spotted Michelangelo's Fiat expertly hidden behind the large tour bus. Edda waved at her from the bus driver's seat as she passed.

Carly scanned the walkway to make sure no one noticed. She approached the Fiat, opened the passenger door and slipped in.

Inside smelled of a hint of masculine aftershave and mint. Michelangelo turned to her with a smile spreading across his luscious lips. He wore a tailored suit, bringing out the curve of his chest and arms. 'Quite an outfit for a gig.'

'It's my disguise.' Carly unwrapped her pink scarf and pulled her arms out of her blazer, stashing her clothes in the back. 'Edda's in on this, too?'

'Let's just say she wanted me to have a night out.'

'She won't tell Ms. Maxhammer?'

'Naw. What's to tell?'

He was right. They weren't going on a date. He was just chauffeuring her to her gig. End of story. 'Okay.' She settled back into her seat and watched the nightlife of Rome flash by in bright lights.

'So, why this gig? What's so important about it?' Michelangelo cast her a curious sideways glance.

Carly debated how much to tell him. He had agreed to teach her Italian and drive her there, so he deserved some explanation. 'If you want to succeed as a freelance musician, you take every gig offered to you.'

'Even in your free time?'

'Ha! Musicians don't have free time.'

He turned a corner, weaving smoothly around the traffic. 'Sounds like a busy life.'

'It is. I spend most of my free time practicing for concerts, or driving to gigs on the weekend.'

'Do you enjoy living this way—as you Americans would say *in the fast lane?*'

Carly shrugged. No one had asked her that before. 'I've lived like this ever since I decided to pursue music in high school. It's the only life I've known.'

'Ah. Sounds like you need to spend a day on a vineyard.' His lips curled suggestively.

Carly shifted in her seat. *Was that an invitation?* She decided to play it cool. 'Why's that?'

'There's nothing like it in all the world. Once you're there, time disappears. Honking cars, people rushing to work, the constant cell phone calls—it's all replaced by buzzing bees, light winds, and the smell of fresh blossoms.'

'I thought you said running a vineyard was stressful.'

He considered her response, drumming his fingers on the steering wheel. 'It is at times, but it's also extremely rewarding.'

Carly recalled the prickle of goose bumps on her skin when she performed a piece of music. 'Guess I'd say the same thing about music.'

'We are at an impasse, then?' He glanced over with a smile.

Wait a sec. Something didn't add up. If he enjoyed the vineyard so much, why did he leave it? 'So why did you leave the vineyard to become a tour guide?'

Michelangelo stiffened and focused on the road ahead.

Carly checked the road, but the traffic was light. Seems she'd hit a nerve.

He rubbed his chin, darkened by light stubble. 'You don't truly appreciate something until you are away from it.'

'Interesting.' Carly thought back to her jobs in the States. Did she miss them? Her constant e-mail checking was more out of necessity than any type of wistful remembering. Then again, she had one of her orchestras over here with her. So, it wasn't the jobs in particular, it was the music.

Michelangelo pulled up to a hotel swankier than theirs, with stone statues of men in togas and white Roman columns strung with ivy. He parked in front of a fluorescent-green Lamborghini and waved the luggage boys away. 'Let me give you my phone number, and you can call me when you're done.'

'Okay.' Carly put his number in under *MR*, just in case anyone saw her phone. Alaina had turned off her alarm the other day; she wouldn't put it past her to skim through her contacts.

'Remember what you learned. Call me if you run into any problems.' He leaned over, and Carly froze in shock.

Michelangelo placed a gentle kiss on her cheek, his lips brushing her skin light enough to send jolts of electricity through her body. 'For good luck.'

So, he kissed me. Don't make a big deal out of it. People kissed on the cheeks all the time in France, right? So was this any different?

She collected her purse and her oboe bag. 'Thank you.'

Michelangelo winked. 'My pleasure.'

CHAPTER ELEVEN

Panic Attack

As Carly slipped through the glass doors of the Cesari Amento, Michelangelo touched his lips, remembering her sweet, soft, skin. He couldn't resist kissing her, yet every logical thought he had screamed to him to let her be.

She'd come too close to the truth tonight, asking why he left his winery to be a tour guide. If he wasn't careful, she'd put two and two together, and then he'd have a lot of damage control to do.

He checked his watch. She'd be done in about three hours, so he had enough time to go back to the hotel and create an alibi.

His phone vibrated, and he checked the caller ID. Ms. Maxhammer.

A vision of poor Edda being tortured by a dominatrix-clad Ms. Maxhammer for information on his whereabouts came to mind.

It couldn't be *that* bad.

He pulled over and answered. 'Hello?'

'Michelangelo? This is Ms. Maxhammer.' Apparently she wasn't aware of caller IDs or was just used to using her name like in the good old dial-up days. Whatever the case, she didn't sound like her normal, cheery self.

'Hello, Ms. Maxhammer. How are you? Is everything okay?'

'Thank goodness I got a hold of you. We have a situation. Please meet me in the lobby as soon as you can.'

Michelangelo looked at his watch as his heart sped into overdrive. 'I'll be there in fifteen minutes.'

Obviously it didn't concern his flirtations with Carly or she'd ask to see him privately. Although he was relieved, he also worried that somehow his tour had taken a dire turn.

He made it in ten minutes and threw his keys to the valet. Ms. Maxhammer stood with a crowd of other orchestra members whispering to each other just beyond the front desk. Everyone's faces were drawn, and one of the violinist's wives had tears running down her cheeks.

They parted before him, and he ran into the circle. 'What happened?'

Ms. Maxhammer leaned on her cane with a grim expression on her face. 'It's Trixie Sanders.'

Trixie? Oh yes, the emo girl who asked him that rude question in the Basilica. 'What about her?'

'No one's seen her since the tour of St. Peters. She and her brother were supposed to meet us back here for dinner.' The violinist's wife, Trixie's mother, grabbed his arm. 'You have to do something.'

A jolt of concern slashed Michelangelo's chest. Yeah, Trixie looked tough, but she was just a little girl in a strange city where boys hid in alleys and stole purses, and worse. At that age, kids thought they lived forever, and all too tragically they were proven wrong. He scanned the crowd. 'What about her brother?'

'I'm here.' Darin moaned from the sofa behind them. Michelangelo approached him. 'Do you have any idea where she went?'

'I already told them I don't.' He wrapped a string from his torn jeans around his finger. 'It's not my fault.'

'You were supposed to watch her.' His mother clutched a picture of a much sweeter Trixie—before the dark makeup, blue hair, and black leather—to her chest.

'Yeah, you try telling her where to go and what to do.' Darin shouted way too loudly for the lobby.

'All right.' Michelangelo put his hands up to stop the argument. What was the normal protocol in a situation like this? He had to come up with something fast. 'The police won't start looking until she's been missing for twenty-four hours. This means we need to search this hotel and the surrounding area.'

He gestured for everyone to circle around him. 'You, you and you check every level of the hotel. You two over there, go next door to the restaurant and see if anyone's seen her. You four, split up in twos and walk down the street in both directions and go in every building you can.'

'What are you going to do?' For the first time since he'd known her, Ms. Maxhammer looked her age. The wrinkles in her face closed in around her eyes, and her cheeks looked dark and sunken in the dim light. He wanted to put his arm around her, like he used to do with his own grandma, and tell her everything was going to be all right. But he couldn't promise anything.

'I'm the only one here with a car.' His mind skimmed through all the possible local hangout spots. 'I'll check every open bar and nightclub within a five-kilometer radius, then keep fanning out.'

He turned to Trixie's parents and placed a reassuring hand on each of their shoulders. Seeing that scraggly thief had triggered all of his memories of Ricco. Many nights he'd looked for Ricco once his father had thrown him out on the street. 'I'll do everything in my power to find her. You stay here in case she comes back.'

Trixie's mom nodded. Her husband held her close and buried his face in her hair. 'Thank you.'

'No need to thank me.' Michelangelo nodded to Ms. Maxhammer, then left for the valet.

If I was a hundred-pound emo teenage girl with problems with authority, where would I go? He waited for the valet to retrieve his car, thinking of all the 'cool' hangout joints.

Emo. Hmmm. He pulled out his phone and Googled *emo bands Rome* with today's date. *Panic Attack* was playing at the Serpent. He Googled the band's website. They had the same sideswept hair as the guys on her shirt. But didn't all those bands look the same?

The club was twenty minutes from the hotel, and a good hour's walk from where he'd last seen her. Michelangelo ran his fingers over the band's faces on his screen. He'd told everyone inside he'd fan out slowly, but a gut feeling told him that's where she'd be.

The valet drove his Fiat right up to the curb, and Michelangelo remembered he'd given his last ten euros to the boy.

'Put five euros on my room number for your tip. I'll sign the receipt when I get back.' Michelangelo hopped in and sped toward the *Serpent*.

Driving through the streets of Rome on a Friday night was like trying to push a pen through a rock. Michelangelo wove his small Fiat around the trucks, swerving as a pedestrian rode a bicycle the wrong way. He knew all of the shortcuts and how to beat most lights. It took him forty-five minutes to reach the nightclub and find a parking spot a block down. He paid the entrance fee with his credit card and walked into the prismatic light spread by a gigantic disco ball.

A slow backbeat emanated from the stage, where a young man sang some sort of whiny ballad about love. A few angst-ridden teens in layered sweatshirts and skinny jeans gave Michelangelo wary looks as he passed. He was way overdressed in his suit, making him look like some type of talent agent or mafia member.

Should have left the overcoat in the car. Some good he'd be in an undercover operation. He ditched the coat on the back of a chair, unbuttoned his shirt, and messed up his hair. Now he looked like some Italian soap opera stand-in, which was more approachable than a mafia hitman.

He scanned the crowd.

Groups of teens loitered by the stage, some of them dancing, and others kissing. Couples sat in booths lining the walls eating fries and drinking beer. Trying not to look too weird, or too old—because a twenty-six-year-old was like ancient history to these kids—he walked the circumference of the room.

Maybe he'd been wrong. A sick feeling spread through his gut. Maybe something had happened to Trixie and she hadn't run off. His pushed those thoughts away. *Just keep looking.*

An oily haired boy wearing a black sweatshirt with an ear full of metal earrings leaned against a column in the corner of the room, blocking the view of the girl he was talking to. He laughed, moving to the side, and lo and behold, there Trixie was, sipping what looked like a margarita.

Bingo. Michelangelo texted Ms. Maxhammer, hoping she'd be able to understand how to open it. He didn't want to cause a scene or draw attention to himself by speaking on the phone. Surprisingly, she texted him back saying they'd be there as soon as possible and to keep Trixie in sight.

The boy put his arms around Trixie, leading her toward a shady hallway backstage. Michelangelo followed them, feeling as though he was in a James Bond movie. They turned into a back room filled with smoke of all kinds and people making out on sofas. A memory of Ricco rolling marijuana in the back of the distillery flashed though his mind.

This had gone too far. No minors drinking and doing drugs on his tour.

Michelangelo approached the pair, cutting in before the boy could offer Trixie anything. 'Excuse me, but I'm going to have to remove this young lady.'

The boy stared at him in confusion, then turned to Trixie. 'Your older brother?'

Trixie crossed her arms, looking as though she could melt him on the spot with her gaze. 'No. My chaperone.'

The boy grinned teasingly. 'Busted.'

Michelangelo stood in between them, blocking the boy with

his back. 'Your parents are on their way. Either they can catch you in here, or outside waiting to be picked up.' He shrugged. 'It's up to you.'

She sucked in her lower lip as she considered his words.

For a second he thought she'd run. 'There's nowhere else for you to go.'

'You think all Americans are delinquents, don't you?' She sneered. 'You think I came all the way to Italy to get high?'

Michelangelo blinked, taken aback. At one point, before this entire tour had started, maybe he had questioned American integrity. After all, they were the ones buying his land to build luxury condos on. But, after meeting so many wonderful, hard-working people—Carly, Bertha, Trixie's parents—he'd changed his mind.

'It's not you I don't trust.' He gestured back into the room. 'It's them.' If Ricco hadn't fallen in with a bad crowd, maybe he'd still be here today.

'Fine. I'll go.' She threw her arms down and walked into the hallway. Michelangelo followed her out of the club to the street corner, where she crossed her arms and pouted. With her head down, only half of one eye peeked out under her slanted blue hair.

Michelangelo checked his watch. It would take her parents another fifteen minutes to get there, so he had to keep her busy until then. 'Don't like the tour?'

She shrugged and tapped her fuzzy Vans on the sidewalk.

He dug into his pocket and offered her a piece of gum.

She looked at it as though it was diseased, then she smirked. 'I don't take candy from strangers.'

Yeah, but she'll take other things. 'Take it. That way they won't smell the alcohol on your breath.'

Gauging him with a new level of respect, she took the gum.

He leaned against a street lamp, trying to look chilled but being ready to run after her at a moment's notice. 'I know Italy's not the most exciting place for someone your age.'

She shrugged. 'It's not that. It's just…my parents always drag me around with them and take me to the places they want to go; they never let me choose, or do my own thing. It's like I'm their little puppy dog.'

Puppy dog was not what he was thinking. More like a crazy kitten. 'You don't look like a puppy dog.'

'You're telling me. I'm practically grown-up—heck I can order alcohol here like all the adults. Yet, they insist on treating me like a baby.'

Edda's tour bus rounded the corner, and Michelangelo breathed with relief. The whole responsible 'dad' thing was a bit premature for him. *Mio Dio*. He needed a girlfriend first. Then he could start to think of marriage, and of having kids running around on the vineyard.

'I'm not going to tell your parents about the drugs or the drink.'

Trixie nodded and bit her lip.

'But I think you're too smart for that shit. Believe me; it can get you into a whole lot of trouble.'

He didn't care if she thought he knew from his own personal experience. He wasn't going to go into detail about his long-lost adopted brother. Teenagers never went for sob stories. 'I want you to think twice next time.'

She nodded distractedly as the bus pulled up. 'Yeah, whatever.'

The doors opened and her parents ran out, throwing their arms around her. Trixie covered her face in embarrassment. 'I'm fine. I'm fine.'

From the bus driver's window, Edda gave Michelangelo a thumbs-up.

As he waved back to Edda, his phone vibrated in his pocket.

Must be Ms. Maxhammer checking in.

The number was unidentified, from the United States.

Carly! He'd almost forgotten.

Feeling like a teen again, Michelangelo ran to his car and tried to curb the excitement rushing through him. Now he'd find out how good a teacher he was.

CHAPTER TWELVE

Anytime

When Carly saw the red Fiat coming to get her, a strange sense of warmth with an edge of exhilaration came over her. She wanted to jump and giggle, and let her hair down so it fell in silken waves down her back.

Michelangelo pulled up and leaned over, opening her door for her. His hair was tousled messily, with curly waves reaching around his ears. He'd unbuttoned his shirt as well, giving her a peek at his smooth, hard, tanned chest. A hot image of him lying in bed naked shot through her mind.

Bad, Carly. Bad.

She slid into the passenger seat, stashing her oboe and her purse behind her.

He smiled as though he hadn't seen her in forever. 'How was the gig?'

'Awesome.' She adjusted her skirt over her legs. *Don't want to show him too much.* 'The violinist said I could come back and play with them anytime.'

'That's wonderful.' Michelangelo turned into the main road. 'And the Italian?'

'Went smoothly, I think.' She laughed. 'Let's hope I didn't say something stupid and not know it.'

'I'm sure you were quite the linguist.'

'All thanks to you.' Blushing, she realized that could have been misinterpreted. She glanced over at his open shirt. Where was his overcoat? Was his sexy toned-down look some type of ploy to seduce her? If so, it was working way too well.

'No. You're a fast learner. Italian seems to come naturally, like you could have lived here in a past life.'

A past life with him? Carly bit her lip. Honestly, her imagination was in hyper-drive tonight. Must have been the after-gig glow.

Change the subject to something safer. 'What did you do?'

Michelangelo sighed, but it seemed more stressful than anything else. 'I've had quite a night.'

'Oh, really?'

He turned toward her. 'Trixie Williams, Bob and Lara's daughter, went missing.'

Although a pang of worry shot through her, Carly wasn't surprised. That girl had trouble clinging to her back. 'She did?'

'Don't worry. We found her.'

She breathed with relief. 'Thank goodness. What a scare.' Bob and Lara had been with the orchestra for a long time and she couldn't imagine the worry they'd been through.

'You're telling me. Looking for her on the streets reminded me of all the nights I spent looking for Ricco.'

Wow, here he was opening up to her again. Were all Italian men this open? 'You really loved him, didn't you?'

'Of course. As a brother. My whole family adored him. I only wish he knew.'

'He knew.' Carly wanted to reach out and touch him, but she commanded her arm not to move. They were getting close to the hotel, and if anyone saw them together, never mind touching, the gossip would fly like wrong notes in a sight-reading session.

The light turned red and Michelangelo turned toward her. 'Why wasn't it enough?'

Whoa. That was a loaded question. Could love be enough to keep anyone from following the path they'd set for themselves? 'I don't know.'

He pulled over a half block away from the hotel. The drive had seemed like mere seconds and it was just getting interesting.

'Why don't you get off here so they don't see us arriving together?'

Getting out of his car was the last thing she *wanted* to do, but the first thing she *should* do. 'Good idea.'

He checked his watch. 'I'll park the car and come in a good twenty minutes after you.'

'Thanks again for doing this for me.' She wished he'd lean over and give her another kiss. But she had nothing she needed luck for. Her gig was over, and so was their time together.

'Sure. No problem. Anytime.' He glanced over with a meaningful look in his eyes.

Carly took her purse and oboe, and closed the door.

Anytime. That sounded like another invitation.

She walked the half block to the hotel remembering Michelangelo's kiss. Her cheek still burned where his lips had brushed her skin. Even though she knew their relationship couldn't go anywhere, she wanted another kiss, and another after that. She hadn't felt this way about any man. Sure, she'd had some experiments in college, but no one made her want him as much as Michelangelo did.

Maybe even more than her music.

Which was why he was so dangerous.

Carly reined in her hormones and walked through the glass doors of the hotel. A bunch of orchestra members hung out in the lobby, whispering excitedly to one another.

Melody spotted her and waved frantically. Carly waved back, albeit with less zeal, and made a beeline toward her friend.

'Carly, where have you been, girl?' Melody pulled her aside to a quiet sofa by the elevators.

'Just taking a walk.'

She scrunched her eyebrows. 'With your oboe?'

Carly looked away, running her hand over her case. 'Yeah, I didn't want to leave it in my room. Lots of hotels have break-ins you know.'

Melody rubbed her chin. 'Gosh, I hope my flute's okay.'

She squeezed her hand, feeling guilty for lying to her best friend and for making her nervous at the same time. 'I'm sure it is. I'm just paranoid, that's all.'

'Boy did you miss all the action tonight.' Melody checked over her shoulder before turning back to Carly. 'Did you hear Bob and Lara's daughter went missing?'

Carly stiffened. If she said yes, then Melody might ask from whom. 'No, really?' She hoped her voice didn't fall too flatly.

'She's okay. Just snuck off with some guy to a nightclub.'

'Wow. They must have been so worried.'

'Yeah, but that's not even the surprising bit. Do you know who found her?'

This time Carly didn't have to lie. Michelangelo had mentioned another specifically. 'Who?'

'The tour guide. He noticed her emo band shirt and looked up all the bands playing in the area. After finding one, he drove off on his own and convinced Trixie to meet her parents outside with no problems.'

'Interesting.' Even though Carly's chest burst with awe, she made sure to keep a straight face. Why hadn't Michelangelo told her? Too modest? Did he know she'd find out from someone else? For some strange, illogical reason, it seemed like what Mr. Darcy did in *Pride and Prejudice* when he found Elizabeth's sister. Now *that* was romantic.

But it was also a long shot. Carly wasn't related to the Williams, and Michelangelo definitely hadn't proposed to her, and this was Italy, not England. So, what he had done was nothing like *Pride and Prejudice* at all.

'He's the best tour guide we could ever have. Boy, does Ms. Maxhammer know how to pick 'em.'

'Right.' Carly stared off into space, trying so hard *not* to swoon again.

'Are you okay?' Melody studied her face. 'You seem withdrawn.'

'Just tired, that's all.'

'Well, I won't keep you up much longer. But I was hoping you noticed.' She raised her left hand, and her ring finger sparkled with a heart-shaped diamond.

Carly's mouth dropped open. 'That's not what I think it is, is it?'

'Mmmhmm.' Melody beamed like she'd just won the best prize in the world.

'Wow. This is so big. The news—I mean. Even though the ring is big, too. This is life-changing.' Carly took her hand, examining the diamond. 'I don't know what to say.' It was final. She really was losing her best friend. She couldn't deny that Melody and Wolf were perfect for each other, but she wasn't ready to give her friend up.

Melody placed a hand on her shoulder. 'Listen, I know what you're thinking, but I'm keeping to the promise I gave you. We can still go out after concerts and have drinks together, just like old times.'

'Sure.' Carly nodded, trying to be happy for her. It would start with one night a month—a girls' night out—then Melody would cancel, and it would become one night every two months, then every six. It had happened to her other friends. *And don't even think about going out if she had kids.*

'I wanted to let you know first, so I waited by the door until you got back.' Melody batted her dark lashes.

A pang of melancholy shot through her chest. *That* was the Melody she knew. 'Thanks, Mel.'

'You'll always be my bff.'

'And you, mine.' Now the guilt came in tidal waves, hitting her conscience with every second. Carly wished she could tell her about Michelangelo, but Melody was now engaged to their boss, of all people, the last person who she wanted knowing anything about her personal life. Hadn't she called Melody out for doing the exact same thing with Wolf when they were first going out? *I'm the biggest hypocrite of them all.*

Carly brought herself back to the reason why they were friends—before Wolf and Michelangelo, even before the East Hampton Civic Symphony. They'd met in school at the New England Conservatory. The intense, competitive atmosphere had weighed on her shoulders, and Melody was the only one who she could blow off steam with. She was the only student willing to give up a night of practice to go out on the town. 'Remember that time back in school when you turned twenty-one and we ordered a whole plateful of margaritas to try out all the flavors?'

Melody laughed. 'I haven't thought of that in years. Boy, we were so new to the world back then. I had no idea what real life as a musician was like.'

'Neither did I.' Carly had always been a hard worker, but never had she thought her jobs would rule her life. Not like they did now. Maybe she needed to blow off a little steam in Italy, before she had a full meltdown. Maybe she needed Melody more than she thought.

She opened her mouth to ask Melody for a girls' night out in Italy when Wolf came into the room. He picked Melody up and whirled her around. 'How's my new fiancée?'

Melody kissed him. 'Happy to share the news.'

He glanced over. 'My apologies, Carly. I didn't see you.'

'That's okay.' Carly stood awkwardly as unease crawled up her legs making her want to get out of there. Can you say third wheel? 'Congratulations. I'm so happy for the both of you.'

Any thoughts of asking Melody to part with her new fiancé flew out the window. 'I really should get going, I have some licks I need to practice before bed.' She tapped her oboe case.

Melody threw her arms around her and squeezed. 'We'll spend

some girl-time together soon.'

Carly left, wondering if Melody could keep her promise, or if she should hold her to it.

I'll just have to find another way to blow off steam.

Darkness greeted Carly as she opened the door to her hotel room. Alaina was sprawled over her bed with every pillow in the room surrounding her. Carly pulled a pillow from under the diva's arm and tossed it back to her own bed, hoping Alaina hadn't drooled on it.

She had a lot to digest. Melody was engaged, Michelangelo was some kind of tour guide superhero, and her Italian gig had gone so well they wanted her back. How she was going to manage that connection from Boston was beyond her imagination, and her budget. But, she wouldn't put it past herself to try.

Climbing under the sheets, she tried to calm herself. Rome's cityscape spread before her in golden lampposts and blinking traffic lights. She was beginning to like Italy and Michelangelo a little too much for her comfort zone. But stopping it was like trying to hold back a tidal wave.

The last thing Carly thought of before the city lights blurred was Michelangelo's kiss.

*****

'Liars! They're liars, all of them!'

Carly squinted against the bright morning sun. An Italian newspaper hovered over her face, until someone tore it away, replacing it with a horrified Alaina.

'Huh?' Carly propped her head on her arm.

Alaina stared at her accusingly. 'I looked all over for Michelangelo last night and couldn't find him, so someone at the reception desk translated the article for me.'

'He was saving Trixie Williams from doing something she'd regret later on.'

Alaina scrunched her eyebrows in a question.

For a moment, Carly thought she might actually care. 'Trixie disappeared after our tour of the Basilica. Can you imagine what her poor parents went through?'

Alain shook the paper. 'Can you imagine what I'm going through? This article is the first Italian review of our aria.'

Carly perked up, then remembered how much the aria sucked. Her stomach sickened. 'Do I really want to know what it said?'

Alaina held up the paper and read from the pen scribbles on the side. 'Signora Amaldi's performance was more like a drowning woman's shriek for help than any ode to love. Her over-the-top vocals and melodrama was only worsened by the oboist's robotic joke of an accompaniment.'

A wrecking ball smashed into Carly's confidence. 'Ouch.'

'My career is ruined.' Alaina collapsed on her bed and buried her head in the pillows, sobbing.

Taking the crumpled paper, Carly reread the article to make sure the man at the front desk had translated it correctly. No one would be *that* nasty, would they?

She struggled with some of the grammar and had to look up a few words on the app on her phone, but Michelangelo had taught her well.

The man at the front desk had translated word for word, if not softening the blow by using 'drowned woman' instead of 'drowned prostitute.' Looked like Carly had some damage control to do before Alaina started demanding a new oboist.

'Listen. Your career is not ruined. We have another performance in Florence tomorrow. We'll practice it again and try different tempos and dynamics. You hire more newspapers to cover the performance, and soon they'll be singing your praises.'

Half of Alaina's face peered out from the pillows. Mascara ran down her cheek to stain the satin sheets. Her nose was as red as her hair. 'You promise?'

'I promise I'll do my best. I can't put words in the critics'

111

mouths. That's up to them.' Hopefully they'd cooperate, or Carly would have to burn every paper in Italy.

'When can we start?'

'What's on the schedule today?'

Alaina checked her pamphlet, sniffling. 'Some tour of a museum.'

Desire panged in Carly's chest. She wanted to see Michelangelo again, even if it was just to hear him ramble on about historical facts. But her career was more important. 'Okay, we'll call Michelangelo and cancel to stay here and practice.'

'You'll do that for me?' Alaina wiped her face.

Carly sighed. Spending the day with Alaina was just about the last thing she wanted to do besides running naked through the streets. 'What are aria buddies for?'

CHAPTER THIRTEEN

Experiments

The ride to Florence from Rome combined three hours of Al's lame jokes with listening to the trombonist complain about missing all the green pigs in *Angry Birds*. Carly checked e-mails, but not as religiously as she had done before. Her eyes kept wandering to the front of the bus, where Michelangelo bared the brunt of Alaina's whining about her bad review.

We'll fix that. They had rehearsed until her hands ached, going through three different reeds until they picked a slower tempo and a gentler dynamic. Carly had coached Alaina on singing in a lighter and more carefree style. Love was all about bonbons and roses, wasn't it? This time they'd have it down. No more bad reviews.

The bus entered the streets of Florence, a smaller, quieter city than Rome. Orange-red tiles covered most of the rooftops, contrasting with the white stucco and stone buildings. As Carly spotted the famous dome of Florence's Duomo, and the site of their next concert, her heart picked up speed.

Michelangelo stood and turned on the intercom. 'Florence is the capital city of the region of Tuscany and the province of Florence. It is considered the birthplace of the Renaissance. It was politically, economically, and culturally one of the most important cities in Europe and the world from the fourteenth to the sixteenth century.'

Alaina tugged on his coat and he abandoned the microphone to talk with her.

Carly sat back in her seat, trying to picture what life was like back when horse-drawn carriages rode the streets, and famous painters like Leonardo, Donatello, Michelangelo—and whoever the fourth Ninja Turtle was—were commissioned to decorate the basilicas they now performed in.

Their bus pulled up beside the massive, white-arched façade of the cathedral, towering so high Carly had to crick her neck to see the top. White, red, and green marble highlighted the geometrical shapes and flower-like decorations.

Michelangelo waved Alaina away, and took up the mic once again. 'Santa Maria del Fiore was built on the site of an earlier cathedral dedicated to Saint Reparata. The ancient building was founded in the fifth century. After undergoing many repairs, Arnolfo di Cambio designed a new church. The first stage of the project would last one hundred and forty years and become the collective effort of several generations. The three great bronze doors depict scenes from the life of Madonna.'

'That looks nothing like Madonna.' Al punched Carly's arm. 'Where's the cone-shaped brassiere?'

Carly shook her head and hid her face in her hands. Sure the Ninja Turtles helped her remember the Italian painter's names, but she wouldn't announce her ignorance to the whole bus.

As the other orchestra members filed off the bus, she took her time, wanting to get a chance to talk with Michelangelo on the way in. She had to warm up for her concert, but just one more thank you for helping her with her gig was in order. As she neared the front of the bus, she thought of all the ways to thank him again without appearing too desperate or tipping off the other orchestra members. She settled on *thanks for all you've done so far.*

Al walked ahead of her, and as he passed Michelangelo he

clapped him on the back. 'Heard about what happened with the girl. Nice save, dude.'

'Thank you.' Michelangelo smiled tightly, then returned to helping people with their bags. Carly wondered if he'd heard Al's sacrilegious comments from the back of the bus.

Al, as always, didn't take the hint. 'Man, you've gotten lucky with the ladies. That Alaina chick is damn hot.'

Michelangelo stiffened. 'I'm not sure what you mean.'

So everyone thinks he's with Alaina? A jealous volcanic eruption went off in Carly's chest. She pushed it down reminding herself it didn't matter because she didn't want an Italian fling.

Al gave him a thumbs-up and grabbed his bag.

Carly froze. After that, she didn't know what to say to Michelangelo. Another thank you would seem like she was trying to make up for what Al had said, or negate it.

Alaina wailed from outside the bus. 'Oh Michelangelo, I need help with my dress bag!'

'Of course.' Michelangelo ran down the steps to help her, leaving Carly alone with Edda.

Carly bristled, digging her nails into her oboe case. Had he ever seen her getting off?

'She's a whiny one, that girl.' Edda shook her head. 'Not his type.'

Carly remembered how Edda had blocked his car so she could get in without being noticed. 'Do you know Michelangelo well?'

She took a sip of her water bottle. 'Well enough to know when he likes someone.' She winked at Carly. 'And when he doesn't.' Edda narrowed her eyes as she glanced toward Alaina's curvy butt as she bent down to pick one of her bags off the ground.

Carly's cheeks grew hot. She grabbed her bag. Was Edda fishing for her reaction? Any comment would give too much away.

'Good luck at your concert.' Edda waved.

Carly turned back and half smiled, half sighed. 'Thanks. I'm gonna need it.'

Gorgeous mosaic floors sprawled before her in dizzying

symmetrical patterns as she entered the cathedral. Her heels clicked, echoing up into the high arched ceilings. No note would go unheard.

Chairs were set up for the orchestra in the main area before the altar. As each player settled in, assembling their instruments, Carly heard a strange whistle from behind.

Michelangelo stood behind a stone column, where only the people entering the church could see him. He gave her a burning *come hither* look and walked back outside to the square.

Carly cast another look at her open principal oboe seat. She needed time to warm up. But a growing desire flamed inside her. She couldn't possibly play the entire concert wondering what he wanted to say.

Making sure no one noticed, she slipped out of the bronze doors. Michelangelo leaned against the façade, waiting for her. Her heart beating wildly, she approached him. 'You wanted to talk to me?'

His eyes traveled the length of her body, then returned to settle into hers. 'I want you to know I'm not with Alaina.'

Carly shrugged trying to look nonchalant. 'It's your business who you're with.'

He grabbed her hand, his skin hot and fiery. 'What if I wanted it to be your business?'

Carly reeled, the square swam before her. She was in Florence, and a gorgeous Italian hottie had nearly come out and said he was into her. The old Carly would have brushed it off, more interested in the gig, but the new her couldn't seem to pull away. *Is this really happening?*

She had to be sure she heard him right. It wasn't every day someone said something to her straight off the pages of a romance novel. 'What do you mean?'

'I keep thinking of the time we've spent together and I need more. I want to get to know you better.'

Carly swallowed a lump in her throat. She felt exactly the same way, but she wasn't about to announce it to him. She dropped his hand and crossed her arms. 'Why?'

Michelangelo sighed. He looked as though he struggled to find the right words. For a smooth Italian hottie, his turmoil over her made him even sexier. 'Because I haven't been able to enjoy myself in a long time, and when I'm with you, I enjoy every minute.'

Was this for real? Or was he sputtering out nonsense just to get her in bed? Carly narrowed her eyes. 'Seems a guy like you could enjoy himself quite a bit in such a beautiful country.'

His gaze faltered as if he was holding back. 'My life hasn't been all rosy Zinfandels and rich Merlots.'

She pretended to be bored, when every ounce of her being wanted to know more. 'You've told me how stressful it is to work in a winery.'

He shook his head and put both hands on her shoulders. 'It's so much more than that—there's so much I need to tell you. Meet me by the rose vase tonight at the Renaissance banquet.'

Carly froze. Did she really intend to go through with this? *Think, Carly, think.* Where would this lead? To another 'experiment'? Did she really want that distraction?

He kissed the back of her hand. 'Please?'

Okay, yes, she did. But could she *afford* a distraction such as this? Was it really worth it?

He still puzzled her, and she wanted to know more about him. Looking into his pleading amber-blue eyes, she found it hard to say no, both to him and to her. A girl's gotta have some fun.

'Okay.'

Before she could swallow the fact she'd just agreed to a secret meeting that wasn't a gig request, Michelangelo bowed his head and ran back to the bus. She checked her watch. The concert started in twenty minutes. Man, he was sly. She had no time to run after him and change her mind.

*****

Michelangelo reached the bus breathless with the sweet scent of Carly's skin still on his mind. After Al's comment about Alaina, he had to do something or he'd lose Carly after he'd worked so hard to win her over.

He had no idea what he was going to say or do at the rose vase, but he had four hours to come up with something. He might just have to trust her and tell her the truth.

Edda teased him with a smile as he got on. 'Had to talk to her again, didn't you?'

He crossed his arms, even though he kinda liked having a mom again. It had been a while since anyone cared about his love life. 'Don't you have other things to do, like check the traffic?'

Edda glanced at her GPS, where she'd taped a picture of her grandson riding a little red train. He had her kind, brown eyes. 'Traffic looks good.'

'Then, let's get to the banquet hall. I have a lot of preparations to make.'

'*Si, signore.*' Edda turned on the engine and Michelangelo took his seat. Strangely enough, his eyes kept wandering to the back of the bus, where Carly had sat. He already saw Al as a rival, so the man's comment about Alaina really irked him. Michelangelo had seen Al make Carly laugh a few times on the way over. Tonight he'd have to do better.

Edda pulled up to the Rosa Rossa hotel, where the orchestra would stay for the night. 'Last stop.' She called over her shoulder.

Michelangelo stood. 'Thanks. Do you think you can pick them up and bring them here without me so I can ensure the banquet goes as planned?' Not only did he need to help with the decorations and oversee the Renaissance-inspired food, he also didn't have the patience to listen to Alaina for another twenty minutes.

'Will do.' Edda turned on the radio to Frank Sinatra singing about accidents and love and winked. 'I like to listen to the oldies when no one's around.'

'You listen to whatever you want, signora.' Wondering what

he'd do without her, he kissed her cheek, then stepped off the bus.

The Renaissance Esperienza touring company was already unloading their trucks of fine fifteenth- and sixteenth-century garments. Michelangelo had made sure to order enough costumes in all sizes. But now he had an idea for a very special one with Carly's name on it…

CHAPTER FOURTEEN

Baroness

The concert flew by in a blur of noise. All Carly could think about was meeting Michelangelo at the Renaissance banquet near the mysterious 'rose vase'. She looked for his alluring face in the audience, but this time she couldn't find him. The aria with Alaina went smoothly, if not a little too smoothly, and she hoped they hadn't overcompensated and *underdone* it this time. But there were other things to worry about. Like what exactly she planned to do with Michelangelo. Or what he planned to do with her…

Disappointment trickled through her as everyone took their seat on the bus and his lay empty. Alaina glanced around eagerly, then abandoned hope and stretched her legs over the seat. If Carly didn't know any better, she would have thought the opera diva liked the spare room more than the hot guy. But Alaina couldn't be *so* self-centered, could she?

The bus pulled up to the Rosa Rossa, a grand five-star hotel right on the River Arno, with roses frescoed onto the stucco walls. As the orchestra members exited the bus, a man in tights with a lute strapped across his back greeted them in Old Italian. Inside the hotel, his female counterpart stood before a rack of costumes for the evening's festivities. Carly got into line, unsure if she liked this new development in the tour.

'This is wonderful!' Melody exclaimed from the front of the line. 'Michelangelo has outdone himself this time!'

'Full name, signorina.' The lady in costume addressed Melody, holding a quill and a sheet of parchment.

'Melody Mires.'

Wolf leaned in, 'Soon to be Melody Braun.'

Melody giggled and Carly squeezed her friend's arm as a tinge of melancholy swept through her. *Already, it's begun.*

The Renaissance woman gave Melody a light-blue high-waisted gown with a silver-threaded bodice.

'It's gorgeous, thank you!' Melody waited for Wolf as he got his own set of leggings and a tailored coat, and the line moved up.

It will be just my luck that my dress is probably hideous, with little pink puffed sleeves and enough stuffing to make my butt look like a tent.

'Name, *mio caro.*' The woman smiled at Carly like a candy-shop owner to a five-year-old.

'Carly Davis.' She tried not to wince.

'Carly Davis?' The woman's eyes brightened. 'Boy do I have something in store for you, courtesy of Michelangelo, of course.' She turned to the rack, shifting through the outfits. 'You are going to be a Baroness tonight.'

'A Baroness? Are you sure?' Was this good or bad?

'Certamente!' The woman pulled out a silken gown of scarlet fabric, embroidered in thick ribbons of gold. Long, bell-shaped sleeves draped to the floor. The outfit came complete with a bejeweled, feathered headpiece.

'My goodness.' Either she'd look majestically glorious or completely ridiculous. She hoped it wasn't the latter.

'I hope mine is that good,' Alaina muttered behind her.

Carly took the dress and walked to the elevator, pressing the number for her floor. She held the fabric up, admiring the hand-stitched work. Michelangelo had requested this dress for her. No matter how she thought of it, the gesture was purely, utterly, swoon-worthily romantic.

'Looks like I got peasant's rags.' Alaina joined her, holding a brown bag of a dress with leather ties that smelled like old cow. 'Wanna trade?'

'Ummm…I'm afraid that isn't my size.' Carly's fingers tightened around the hanger. She wouldn't put it past the diva to try and outshine everyone—wearing Carly's dress. The elevator opened and both ladies stepped in.

Alaina stood a little too close to her, breathing down her neck as if to smell Michelangelo's cologne on her skin. 'Why would he give you a special dress?'

'I don't know.' Carly backed into the wall to get more space between them. After telling Alaina that Michelangelo was all hers, agreeing to meet him secretly would make her the biggest two-faced liar in the orchestra.

Alaina's eyes stared, like her rendition of Mozart's evil *Queen of the Night*. 'You don't know?'

'Maybe I won a raffle? You know, he pulled my name out of a hat or something.'

'Mm-hmm.' Alaina pulled a tattered thread off her ugly dress and dropped it to the floor.

Unfortunately, the roommates were fixed for the entire trip.

The elevator beeped and the door opened.

'What room are we looking for?' Alaina didn't even bother to check her own paperwork.

Thank goodness she'd dropped the dress issue. Sopranos were known for their short attention spans. 'Five sixty-two.'

'Right.' Alaina ran her fingers through her silky red hair. 'I forgot to tell you, the other day, Michelangelo showed me to this wonderful little café.'

'He did?' Carly's heart missed a beat. Was he playing them both? Making them fight for him against one another like dogs?

124

'Yeah. I was walking to this other one, *the Picasso Café*. But Michelangelo was just coming out and he told me the food wasn't so good, so he showed me to the *Bel Piatto* down the street.'

So, he had two dates in a row? Carly tried to control her jealousy, but it was like holding a raging pit bull by the collar. Didn't like the food, eh? He seemed to enjoy his panini just fine.

'He didn't sit with me, he had tour stuff to do. But still, it was such a romantic gesture.'

'Oh, I see.' Had he driven Alaina away from discovering them? Or was he really wooing them both? Carly didn't know him as well as she thought. Sure, he was open about his past on the vineyard, but four days of touring Italy was hardly enough to decipher any kind of character, or at least, not enough for another 'experiment' in her book.

What if she didn't meet Michelangelo at all? That would certainly cool down what they had going and keep her on task. But stiffing him would be the easy way out, and she'd always wonder about him after going home. No, he was too irresistible to let go of so easily.

She'd have to confront Michelangelo about Alaina at the rose vase. He'd probably vehemently deny any relationship, as he'd done in the past. But Carly wasn't going anywhere with him, both location-wise or physically until he gave her some substantial answers.

*****

Michelangelo strapped on his breastplate, admiring the golden dragon insignia on the front. *Mio Dio*, Renaissance women's outfits looked much more comfortable then men's. But it was either that or tights, so the heavy armor would have to do for the night. What he *was* looking forward to was seeing Carly in that gorgeous baroness dress he'd picked out. Just thinking of the way the red fabric would cling to her slight curves stirred desire deep in his gut.

Some things were worth it. Besides, he wanted the Easthampton

Civic Symphony to have the night of their lives. They were certainly paying him enough for it. Besides a few choice members, he was beginning to like them, and he felt more and more of a responsibility to earn every euro of his check.

He slung his plastic sword into the sheath on his belt. Tonight would be easy. The tour company had all of the talking covered. So, all he had to do was show his face, then meet Carly at the rose vase in the back antechamber.

Whistling, he left his room in high spirits and took the elevator down to the banquet hall. Members of the orchestra were already filing into their seats while servants dressed in tunics brought jugs of wine and carried trays of appetizers, including cheese and biscuits, small meat pies, and fruit pastries. But he wasn't hungry for *food* tonight. He hungered for something else. Scanning the room, he looked for Carly's grand scarlet gown.

'My, you look dashing tonight, hon.'

Michelangelo turned and saw Bertha and her friend—*what's her name…oh yes, Trudy*—admiring him like two bachelorettes in a men's strip bar. They were dressed as Renaissance nuns, complete with the brown robe and white muslin cowl collars, with a white cord tied around their waists.

Trudy reached out with her hand. 'I just want to pinch your—'

Michelangelo cleared his throat. 'Ladies, please have a seat. A servant will be with you shortly.'

'Yes, signore. Or is it Sir Michelangelo?' Bertha laughed.

'That has a certain ring to it.' He showed them to their seats and told their table server to go light on the wine.

Embarrassment creeping up his neck, Michelangelo walked over to Ms. Maxhammer.

Ms. Maxhammer stood from her seat at the head of the table looking regal in a navy-blue Queen's gown. A bejeweled plastic crown sat amongst her gray curls. Instead of a cane, she held a scepter. 'Michelangelo! This is all so wonderful. What a great idea for the tour!'

He bowed like a knight before his queen. 'Thank you. It's my pleasure. I hope you and the orchestra enjoy the evening.' Out of the corner of his eye, he saw a flash of red satin and gold. His heart leapt.

'They will, and they certainly deserve it.' Ms. Maxhammer gestured for him to stand. She sat down and folded her napkin across her lap.

'I have to agree with you. They've been working hard.' His gaze strayed across the room and he stifled a gasp in his throat. Carly broke through the crowd, looking tantalizingly amazing in her gown. She'd pinned up her blonde hair in swirls around her bejeweled headpiece, so only a few strands dangled just beyond her ears. Ears he wanted to nibble.

'And sounding incredible.' Ms. Maxhammer's comment brought Michelangelo back to reality. He thought of Carly's oboe-playing and pointed to Ms. Maxhammer as though she'd hit the nail on the head. 'You're right there. They are excellent players.' Even if Carly didn't think so.

He kissed the back of Ms. Maxhammer's hand. 'If you'll excuse me, Your Highness, I have to be getting around to the other guests.'

She offered him a sly smile. 'Of course.'

Michelangelo turned toward Carly and their eyes met like two jolts of electricity converging. He stood, breathless as her presence rippled through him, rocking his world. The intensity of her gaze sent warmth throughout his body. She must have been thinking of their secret meeting.

His pocket vibrated. He was still on duty, so to speak, so he checked the caller ID. Isabella. She hadn't contacted him in a while, and at this time of night it had to be an emergency.

Michelangelo bowed his head to Carly and rushed through the banquet hall for privacy. The last ring emanated from his hand as he wove through the chairs in the back. He turned the corner and took the call. 'Ciao, Isabella, is everything all right?'

'You've got to get over here, pronto!' Her voice shook with

anxiety, shattering his composure.

'Why? What's wrong?'

She stifled a sob. 'I spent most of the day in the packaging department, shipping out crates. When I returned to the office, I saw them on the ridge.'

A thousand scary images came to mind: men with guns, a swarm of pests, grape-eating goats, aliens…' Who, what?'

'The tractors. They're here all in a row. They're set to demolish the northern field in the morning. If you don't do something, there'll be no winery to save.'

Michelangelo threaded his hand through his hair and tugged on the roots until his whole head hurt. 'I thought they said we had another month.'

'Herb Ranger is out there now, taking measurements.'

Herb Ranger. The American contractor and all-round *idiota*. He'd offered the Ricci family millions when Michelangelo was just a child, and his father refused to be bought out. He could still hear his father's slow and calm voice of reason. *This is my son's land, and his son's after him. You cannot put a price on heritage.*

Well, apparently, Herb could. He just had to wait until the old man passed away and a few droughts ravaged the land.

Michelangelo bunched his palms into fists. 'Don't let them move. I'm leaving Florence now and I'll be there in three hours.'

'Hurry.' Isabella hung up.

Michelangelo took one last longing look at the banquet. Everything was set up, all he had to do was text Ms. Maxhammer, saying he'd meet them in Milan and that he'd gone early to make preparations. But as for Carly, there was nothing he could do. If he confided in her, he'd blow his cover. If he tried any other excuse, he'd look like an *idiota*.

Frustration boiled through his veins as he ran from the building to his car. This was the story of his life, and the reason why he'd never been able to keep up any relationship longer than a week. The winery always came first. He'd been a fool to think he could support a new relationship as well.

Say arrivederci to love.

*****

Ravenous desire had spread like wildfire inside of Carly as she locked eyes with Michelangelo in his dashing knight's ensemble. His usually wavy hair had been pulled back, revealing the exquisite angles of his cheeks and the sharp amber-blue of his eyes. He was dressed to steal some hearts, with hers first on the list. For a moment, she felt like a real Renaissance princess, greeting the knight who had come to her balcony after a tragic battle. What was happening to her? She'd never been the girl fantasizing about a man. Fantasying about a solo, or a monumental gig perhaps.

Come on, girl, get a grip.

Michelangelo had looked down at something in his hand. His face stiffened. Distractedly, he bowed to her and took off across the room as though the end of the world had arrived. Her imminent desire sputtered and cooled.

WTF? Was she wearing the dress incorrectly? Or had he chickened out like the biggest commitment-phobe on the planet?

Relax. Probably had an emergency and would return shortly. Maybe they'd run out of wine.

She scanned the tables for her name and found her seat, next to Al of all people. He turned and the bells on his triple-pronged jester hat jingled. The bright red and orange on his checkered tunic almost blinded her.

'Damn. You look hotter than a hot potato.' He pulled out the seat next to him. 'My lady.'

'Thanks, Al.' She checked the door, but there was no sign of Michelangelo returning. 'So what's on the menu?'

'Renaissance shit.' Al passed her a loaf of bread that weighed as much as a rock. 'Good luck cutting a piece.'

'Thanks.' *Oh so chivalrous.*

As Ms. Maxhammer began a speech about the orchestra's progress and Wolf's great talent for raising money, Carly's mind drifted back to the door, which Michelangelo had disappeared through. Annoyance turned to concern. What could possibly have taken him away from his job and meeting her?

Alaina snuck in late, plopping into the seat next to Carly in her peasant's rags. She looked as though she could play Fantine in the next *Les Miserables* performance.

Carly leaned over and whispered, 'What happened to you?'

'Mortification. That's what.' Alaina pulled out her iPad, making sure Ms. Maxhammer didn't notice. 'We got our first review.'

'What?? Already? But the papers haven't even come out yet.'

'This reviewer has a blog and he posted right after the event.' She clicked on the internet icon on her iPad. 'This thing translates the Italian into English.'

She clicked on the saved link and handed Carly the iPad.

Carly's fingers shook as she read the column. 'The Overture was charming and energetic…' blah blah blah. She scrolled down to where she saw the word *Aria*.

'…the aria, on the other hand, was a complete bore. I have a hard time believing either of those ladies has ever loved anyone enough to sing about love, never mind marriage.'

Carly took her napkin and scrunched it into a ball. 'He can't be serious.'

Alaina nodded. 'He is totally serious, and one of the most renowned classical music reviewers in Florence.'

'So I've never been in love. So what? I can still play eighth and sixteenth notes.'

'Well, I've loved many times.' Alaina leaned back in her chair luxuriously, a slit in her dress that hadn't been there when Carly last saw it on the hanger exposed her upper thigh. 'Many. Times.'

Al drooled. 'Is that so?'

'Loved and being in love are two different things.' Carly threw her wad of a napkin on her plate.

Alaina's face fell as if Carly had punched her in the gut. She took a swig of her wine and glanced down sullenly at her empty plate.

So the diva's never been in love. Guilt trickled through Carly. She shouldn't have said anything. Michelangelo's disappearance had put her in a vile mood, making her speak insensitively. Even if Alaina was bitchy at times, she didn't deserve to have Carly make her feel like a slut.

Carly pulled her chair closer to Alaina's. 'We'll do better next time, I promise. Obviously we were too subtle this time. We need to find a balance between too much and too little.'

Alaina chugged the rest of her ale. 'Or we should just face it: this aria is doomed.'

Carly never failed at anything musical. This tour was not going to be the exception. 'It's not doomed. We'll practice it another way. We still have one more concert.'

'And one more chance to embarrass ourselves,' Alaina sighed.

Al leaned over Carly's lap, leering at Alaina. 'Drown your sorrows with me, babe. I can be one of those *many times*.'

Alaina stared at him as though he'd grown another jester prong on his head. 'I happen to be involved at the moment.'

'Oh yeah? With a certain Michelangelo?' Al emptied his mug.

Alaina set down her glass. 'Just because I've never been "in love" before doesn't mean I'm not looking for it rather than just some one-night stand.'

Carly pushed her rock-hard bread away. Musicians and alcohol just didn't mix. Between Al's lewd jokes, the bad review, inadvertently calling Alaina a slut, and Alaina's suggestion of her relationship with Michelangelo, she'd lost her appetite.

'Where is the knight in shining armor right now?' Alaina scanned the room wistfully.

'He left suddenly. Guess he had an emergency.' Carly couldn't keep the suspicion from her voice.

Thankfully, Alaina was too into her own feelings to notice it. 'Awww. Poor guy. I hope he figures it out soon and comes back to us.'

Al chuckled beside her. 'I hope not.'

Servers brought out roasted pheasant, grilled venison, and sautéed root vegetables. Carly could barely eat two bites. Her mind brimmed with questions about Michelangelo. Was he the knight in shining armor that he dressed up as? Or was it all a ruse?

After dinner, everyone gravitated toward the dance floor, where the Renaissance touring company taught the slow, stately dances of the *pavane*. Carly walked around the tables to the back room, where an oversized rose vase as tall as she was held gigantic ferns.

She tugged a fern down, feeling the leaf under her fingertips. Plastic. Fake. Was Michelangelo the same?

Two voices came from the banquet hall, and Carly hid behind the vase, afraid someone would see her pruning the ferns.

'Personally, I don't think he's a great tour guide at all. I mean, his knowledge of the areas we passed was minimal at best, and he got the date of St. Peter's Basilica wrong.'

Carly stiffened. That was Reena Kempt, a cellist. She excelled in proving other people wrong. Usually her offhand criticisms annoyed Carly, but this one hit a nerve.

'Really? I don't know anything about Italy, so I have had no idea.' The other lady was Reena's friend, Macie, a violist. String players always seemed to stick together, as though the other sections of the orchestra were second-class citizens.

'Yeah. He even made up some story about a secret society called the Brotherhood of the Manifesto. I looked it up, and there's nothing about it in any of my sources.' Reena sounded as though his misinformation personally offended her. If Carly hadn't already had suspicions about him then she would have thought his invention kind of funny. But, under the circumstances, it only worsened her burgeoning fears that her knight in shining armor was a knave in disguise.

'Either he's a complete genius who knows more than the history books, or he's making stuff up to keep you on your toes.' Macie laughed.

'A tour guide should only give out facts.' Reena crossed her arms. 'Come on, let's see how accurate their dance steps are. I've taken a few Renaissance dance classes myself.'

As both women walked away, Carly leaned against the wall, chewing her lower lip and remembering all the times Michelangelo had glanced down before talking into the intercom on the bus. If he'd done a bunch of tours, why was he so nervous? Did he have some sort of cheat sheet in his hands? And in the car, when she asked him why he quit the winery to be a tour guide, he gave her some sort of vague, philosophical response. At the time, it hadn't bothered her, but with all this new evidence, something smelled fishy, and it wasn't the Renaissance food.

Not only was Michelangelo slippery in his dealings with her and Alaina, but he was also hiding something about being a tour guide. She'd have to get to the bottom of it, not only for herself, but for everyone in the orchestra.

One thing was for sure: Michelangelo wasn't to be trusted.

CHAPTER FIFTEEN

Big Plans

Michelangelo sped all the way to his vineyard on the outskirts of Milan. If Herb had already driven the tractors there, then the situation was worse than he'd thought. How could his American landlords sell them out so quickly? He'd told Michelangelo there'd be a grace period of a few months. Unless Herb had given the landlord an offer he couldn't refuse.

Which was likely, knowing Herb.

His blood boiled in his veins and his fingers tightened around the steering wheel. He had to exert enormous self-control to keep himself from driving his Fiat into the ground.

Hours later, he turned into the long, windy driveway that led to his family's estate. It was now approaching nine o'clock, and he couldn't imagine any tractor drivers working at this late hour. Hopefully, Isabella had stalled Herb enough so they hadn't done any damage. To lose the newest section of vines he and his father had planted together would be like losing his father all over again.

The shrubs along the roadway had overgrown, narrowing the road and scraping against the side of his car. Usually his family had a landscaper trim them, but now he'd have to do it himself.

He turned the corner, and rows and rows of trellises threaded with green vines came into view. Relief poured over him along with a strong melancholy. Many days he'd spent playing hide and seek with Ricco in those seemingly never-ending rows. He hadn't realized how much he'd missed being home.

His chest tightened as he scanned the horizon. Dark shapes lurked on the top of the hill, where he'd installed a cobblestone patio and lounge chairs for his parents to watch the work in the fields. Isabella had not been exaggerating. Seeing the wreckage trucks with their sharp-toothed plows made the whole problem more real.

He parked in the circular drive and entered the office part of his family's estate, a small addition built onto the stone foundation of the old house.

Isabella sat at the desk, poring over paperwork. Her belly had grown so round she had to reach her arms out to type at the computer.

'Isabella, what are you still doing here?'

His secretary glanced up and relief filled her dark eyes. 'Making sure Herb doesn't get trigger-happy. But now I see a knight in shining armor has come to save the day.'

Michelangelo shook his head, looking down at his costume. He must look ridiculous, as though he'd sold his soul to entertaining silly Americans. 'Is he still here?'

She nodded. 'Sitting on your parents' swing by the apple trees and writing down some sort of plan. I told him not to move an inch until he talked to you or I'd call the police.'

Michelangelo balled his hands into fists. How dare Herb use the swing his father had proposed to his mother on to record information about demolishing the vine fields?

'I'll go talk to him.'

Isabella pursed her lips. 'You'd better.' She gave him a stack of papers. 'I've been looking through all of the legal documents. When your dad remortgaged the winery to pay for the extra fields, he made a contingency amendment in case of bankruptcy. We are still in our grace period. Herb has no power until the end of next week. No legal power, anyway.'

Michelangelo took the stack of papers. 'Okay, I'll see what I can do.'

He turned toward the patio, but movement from the corridor behind him caught his attention.

'Someone bring me my slippers. It's raining, and my feet are cold.'

Unconditional love followed by a wistful ache spread through him. 'You're wearing your slippers, mamma.' Michelangelo shot over and helped the frail waif of the woman his mother had become down the corridor, steering her back to her room. Where was her nurse? How did she get all the way to the office? He checked her arms to make sure she didn't have any bruises from falling or bumping into the railings. Her skin was so flaky it could blow away with the wind. He'd have to instruct Lila to apply more moisturizer. Guilt panged his chest. He'd been away for too long.

As he took her arm, she looked at him with suspicion. 'Who are you?'

'I'm you son, mamma. Michelangelo, remember?'

A moment of tension squeezed his heart before her eyes softened. 'Ah, yes. Tell your father to get in before dark. He shouldn't be working in the rain.'

Michelangelo blinked back tears. It was easier to go along with her than have her discover her husband had passed away again and again. 'I will. Let's get you back to your room.'

Lila rushed down the stairs. The middle-aged nurse had pulled her graying black hair in a bun. Dark circles rimmed her eyes. She looked five years older than when he last saw her. 'Oh, *Grazie a Dio*! I went to the bathroom for five minutes and she disappeared.'

'It's okay. I've got her.' Michelangelo took his mother's left arm while Lila took the other. His mother was hard to care for, and he hoped Lila wasn't thinking about quitting like the last three nurses.

Sure, he could put his mother in a home, but he really believed the winery helped her retain some of her memories. To take her out of where she'd spent the majority of her life would speed up the progression of the Alzheimer's. He just couldn't do it.

They put his mother to bed, and Michelangelo tucked her in, kissing her forehead.

She grabbed his hand, her grip surprisingly strong. 'Where's Ricco? I haven't seen that boy in a long time.'

This time, Michelangelo couldn't play the game. 'He left remember?'

She nodded. 'Your father should have never kicked him out.'

'I know.' But it was senseless trying to go back and fix the past. That's why it was hard to be with his mother, because that's all she talked about. The past was her only reality now.

'You find him for me. Tell him to come home.'

'I'll try, mamma.' He squeezed her hand, then joined Lila in the hall.

Lila closed the door slowly, leaving it open just a crack. 'She's been acting up lately. I think she senses the tension with everything going on.'

'Of course. You are doing a wonderful job. It's me who has to step up to the plate.'

Guilt hit him hard in the gut. How could he be romancing Carly at a time like this? When he got back to his tour job, he'd have to tone it down if he was ever going to save this place and his mother.

'Nonsense.' Lila gave him a stern look. 'You're working hard to keep everything together.' She patted his arm. 'You're doing just fine. I know you'll figure something out. Things have a way of working themselves out.'

He wished he had her certainty. 'I'd better. If not, I won't be able to afford the best care for my mother, and she's just getting worse.'

'She comes back to us now and then on the days she's feeling well enough to take a walk outside. Then, I get a glimpse of the

138

passionate and strong-willed woman who raised you so well.'

*On the days she walks outside…*even more reason to believe moving her would only accelerate her condition. He had to keep the winery. 'You're right about that. She was strong, sometimes too much so.' He leaned against the wall. He knew Herb was waiting, but he wanted to relay this one particular story to Lila to show her how much fire his mother once had. 'Once, she told off a customer who'd complained about the quality of the wine—she said they couldn't tell Chardonnay from Merlot.'

Lila laughed. 'I bet she did.'

'Not only that, but she told the staff not to sell them any more wine. Said they didn't deserve it.'

'Now that's what I call a healthy dose of pride.'

Michelangelo could still see his mother for what she had been, and not the ghost of a person she was now. 'Thank you for taking care of her.'

The older woman nodded, smoothing all of the stray wisps of hair around her face. 'I do my best. Now you'd better get down to the patio before Herb-money-pockets decides to put those tractors to use.'

'I will.' He glanced back through the crack in the door at his mother. Her breathing had slowed and steadied. At least she slept soundly.

Michelangelo waved to Isabel as he walked back through the office. 'You go home and get some rest. I'll handle this.'

'Si, signore.' She shut down the computer and wiggled her finger in the air. 'You stick to your ground. Remember, he's not supposed to be on this property until his end of the deal is signed.'

He waved the paperwork. 'Thank you for looking into it.'

She smiled, lifting a lunch bag to her shoulder. 'That's my job.'

He'd recovered some of his composure after seeing his mother. He hadn't driven for three hours for nothing. He would end this one way or another.

Michelangelo walked across the patio toward the apple trees.

Maybe it was the brightness of the moon, or the feeling that his world was falling apart, but more of the tiles seemed cracked and broken. He made a mental note to call a mason, *if* he didn't lose the property.

'Lovely night.' Herb spoke in his lazy southern-American accent and tipped his cowboy hat. He had the charming roundness and inviting smile of Santa Claus, which Michelangelo always thought was misleading.

'It is.' Michelangelo crossed his arms. 'Although, I'm not sure why you're here.'

'Hey, now, don't get your plastic sword all up in a twist. The landlord said I could store these here since I'll be closing on a deal with him by the end of next week—that's if you can't come up with the money. So, I'm just coming to inspect my property and make sure it's all working up to speed.'

Michelangelo tensed. Did he mean testing it out?

'Come to stop me, eh?'

'Yes, I have.' Michelangelo's tone meant business, and Herb dropped his comical friendliness.

'Listen, son.' He put a hand on Michelangelo's arm. 'You know I've been eyeing this property for some time.'

Michelangelo shrugged his arm off.

Herb picked a blossom from the apple tree and sniffed it. 'It's a beautiful piece of Italy, and could make a lot of my oil-tycoon friends in Texas very happy. The winery's had its days of glory. But let's face it: the estate is run-down. It's not making the same money as it used to, and who's gonna run it? A daft old widow.'

Michelangelo stepped toward him. 'Don't talk about my mother like that.'

Herb raised both his hands in apology. 'I'm just speaking the truth.'

'I'm going to run it, Mr. Ranger,' Michelangelo growled. 'And I'm going to turn this place around.'

Herb nodded as if he'd predicted this. 'I know your daddy had big plans. But do you really want to spend your youth toiling over a bad investment? All good things must come to an end. Why not end it now and walk away?'

Michelangelo sighed. Was he here to preserve his family's heritage because that's what his dad had wanted? Or was he following his own dream? Driving back up here had reminded him of everything he loved about the vineyard. He'd missed the place just like he missed an old friend. Being a farmer like his father had always been his childhood dream. He'd never wanted to leave. Even if he found a job in the city, he'd always pine for the rows of green and the buzzing of the insects.

The winery ran in his blood, and it was an urge he couldn't ignore.

'I'm not going to do that, signore.' He crossed his arms. 'I'm going to find a way to buy this land. I could call the authorities, but I thought we could handle this man to man.'

Herb kicked a chipped tile. 'I'm listening.'

'I'll offer you this: Give me the time allotted to find the money for this month, and if I don't come up with it, I won't give you any problems when the deal closes. But in the meantime, stay off my winery.'

'Fair enough.' Herb nodded and his smile sent a chill through Michelangelo's heart—as though he'd just made a deal with the devil.

CHAPTER SIXTEEN

Locked Heart

'Man, do I have a meat hangover today.' Al clutched his stomach as he moved over so Carly could take her seat beside him on the bus. She still hadn't been able to switch with anyone despite her constant pestering—which said a lot about Al.

He studied her face. 'So what happened to Mr. Romeo?'

'You mean Michelangelo?' It was hard to say his name without wincing.

'Yeah, our "dreamy" tour guide.' He said the word *dreamy* in a high-pitched voice like a teenage girl.

She shrugged as Edda pulled the bus away from the hotel. 'I'm guessing he had some emergency.'

An older violinist turned around in her seat. 'I heard from Ms. Maxhammer he'd gone to Milan early to make preparations for our tour of the Galleria tomorrow and our next concert on Tuesday. She said he'd join us there.'

Interesting. If he'd planned to go anyway, why did he run out of the banquet in such a rush? Had something gone wrong with the planning and he was trying to smooth it out before they got there? Or was it something worse? A bigger secret he was hiding

143

from them all.

'Was there a problem with our reservation?' Carly tried to keep her suspicion from her tone.

The older woman shrugged. 'Not that I know of.'

'See, what you need is a guy like me, someone who stays in the same seat with you on the bus.' Al grinned.

Carly gave him a nasty look. She couldn't have him thinking she was interested in Michelangelo, and she also couldn't have him believing she was available. 'I thought you were into Alaina, and before that, the girl at the front desk at our first hotel.'

He winked. 'Today I'm into you.'

'Oh shove it up your trombone.'

His face paled. 'Geez, I was only kidding.'

She pulled out her phone and responded to e-mails as they drove to Milan. *Women Reeds* were doing surprisingly well without her. They had a few concerts with just flutes and clarinets, and the second-in-command was handling all of the press and program printing. Carly's students all had their own vacations and summer music camps, and no e-mails from Dino. She did have an e-mail from Mario, however, asking her if she'd be available to play future gigs with the Italian chamber orchestra in Rome.

As Carly considered his offer, and how in the hell to get to Rome from Boston, they reached the sprawling city of Milan. Looking much more modern than Rome and Florence, Milan had glassy skyscrapers and other office buildings scattered through the ancient streets. They pulled up to the Galleria and Michelangelo stood waving on the curb.

A mix of distrust, excitement, and wistful longing erupted inside her, and she could barely keep herself sitting still in her seat as the doors opened and he walked up the steps to the intercom.

'Greetings, my dear orchestra friends. Welcome to Milan, the second-largest city in Italy. This city was founded by the Insubres, a Celtic people, and later conquered by the Romans. Milan is the main industrial, financial, and commercial city of Italy, and is also the home of the Italian stock exchange, the Borsa Italiana.'

He glanced down at his hand as he had done before, and Carly wanted to jump out of her seat and turn his palm over to see what was there. Didn't anyone else notice, or were they all so taken by his charm they didn't care?

Michelangelo's eyes fell on her, and he quickly looked away. 'The Galleria Vittorio Emanuele II is the oldest shopping mall in Italy. It is named after the first king of the Kingdom of Italy and originally designed in 1861 and built by Giuseppe Mengoni between 1865 and 1877.'

Carly glanced over to Reena to see if she had any violent reaction to his dates, but the cellist sat calmly with her hands folded in her lap.

Guess he got those facts correct.

Michelangelo gestured toward the door. 'Follow me and you'll have the shopping experience of your lives.'

Because Al had chosen the window seat, he followed Carly down the aisle. There would be no time to confront Michelangelo about his disappearance the previous night. Any allusion to their meeting would certainly draw attention.

As they filed off the bus, Michelangelo locked eyes with hers. As hard as she looked, she couldn't understand the complexity of his gaze. It was something like guilt mixed with hope. But something else as well, something he was hiding.

As she walked past him, he slipped his hand into hers and left a small piece of paper. 'Hope you enjoy the tour.'

Carly nodded, unable to react to his note in front of Al. Apprehension bubbling inside her, she stepped off the bus and walked toward the Galleria. As she unfolded the note, she turned her back to the other orchestra members toward the grand arched entrance to the shopping mall. The crowd of people entering and leaving was more than enough to hide her hands and discreetly read the note.

His handwriting was gorgeous, with strong, sure strokes. *My apologies for last night, there was a last-minute emergency that had to be taken care of. No worries. All is well.*

She turned the note over, but nothing else was written on it. No further explanation or request to meet. Had he changed his mind about her?

Disappointment trickled through her even as she told herself it was all for the best. He was probably some playboy tour guide womanizer more interested in the ladies than the actual history and dates. If she was at all sane, she'd stay away from him.

They entered the Galleria, and Carly stared up at the arched glass ceilings. The midday sun shone through, illuminating the four-story building façades and mosaic-tiled floor. The luxurious storefronts of Prada, Gucci, Louis Vuitton, and Swarovski lined the walkways. It was nothing she needed or could afford, but pretty to look at nonetheless and a great way to get her mind off Michelangelo and the looming concert, which was her and Alaina's last chance to prove themselves on that ridiculous aria.

Michelangelo began reciting historical facts about the Galleria, taking them on a full tour before going into the shops. They stopped at the mosaic tile in the center, where it was custom to spin your heel on the bull.

While the orchestra members took turns spinning their heels, Michelangelo snapped pictures. Carly wandered off to window shop, trying her best not to entangle herself further into Michelangelo's schemes. Even if she was thankful for him teaching her Italian and driving her to her gig, her gratitude had to stop there. Sure, she had a pull toward him that she'd never had with any man before, but her playing and her career was more important.

She walked up to a jewelry store with giant diamonds and rubies shaped like hearts in the front window. The retailer inside wore a finely tailored suit. He glanced up at her as she browsed, with interest in his eyes.

Nope, not going in there.

She walked over to the next shop, which was selling leather

purses.

Even if she and Michelangelo had gotten together, it would lead to more heartbreak in the end when she returned home. All this was definitely for the best.

She glanced over to the center of the Galleria. The orchestra had moved on, and Michelangelo stood beside a café, explaining how the founder in 1867 was the pastry chef to the monarch.

She gravitated toward the edge of the group, listening in. Michelangelo had a waitress come out of the café with a tray of white pastries with cherry glaze in the center. As the orchestra each sampled one, he stepped aside. Alaina pushed to the tray like a vulture after roadkill. She'd be occupied for the next five minutes at least.

Carly's heart sped. *Stay where you are, young lady! No, go ask him about the emergency.* Really, it would be rude not to. As much as his strange behavior made her question him, she couldn't help feeling indebted, annoyed, and just a little intrigued. Besides, she had to look out for the orchestra, and if there was something he wasn't telling them, he could be conning Ms. Maxhammer out of a lot of their tour fund money.

Now was her chance.

She wiggled her way over to the tables outside the café. Michelangelo took a seat at one, checking something on his phone. He glanced up at her, and his face hardened as if she was a matter he wasn't prepared to deal with. He shut off the screen to his phone and slipped it into his pocket. 'Ms. Davis.'

She took the seat next to him, wondering every second why she was doing it. 'I trust everything went okay last night?'

'Yes, yes. Just a small inconvenience.' His fingers drummed along the table. 'My apologies again.'

An awkward silence fell between them. *Now what, Einstein?* Carly had gone over there for answers, and answers were what she'd get.

She steeled her nerves. 'Why did you tell Reena that the

Brotherhood of the Manifesto built St. Peter's?'

A small smile curved in his lips. 'She mentioned it, eh?'

Carly contained her own smile. It was funny, even if it wasn't true. 'She looked it up, and she's not too happy about the results.'

He traced a circle with his finger on the table. 'Well, maybe she didn't use the right source.'

Fair enough, but she wasn't going to let him get away without other answers. She grabbed his hand and turned over his palm. The skin on the other side was clean, with nothing written on it.

He raised an eyebrow in a look that said *you really want to do this here*?

She dropped his hand again before anyone saw. 'What do you keep looking at in your hand when we're on our trips?'

Michelangelo shifted in his chair and breathed in slowly. 'That is not your concern.'

'What about keeping your appointments?'

He put both arms on the table and rubbed his temples. 'Listen, I'm sorry about asking you to meet me and then not being there. And I'm sorry I led you on. I really do like you…a lot.' Intensity flared in his eyes. 'Too much. But we both know this isn't the time for romance, whether we want it or not.'

Carly blushed. Her words stuck in her mouth. *Romance? He likes me a lot?* She couldn't believe this Casanova was the one pulling away, calling it quits before the fun had even started. Heck, he'd almost had her, and now this? None of it made sense.

'B-but—'

The waitress came over with the empty tray. '*E finite, signore.*'

He slipped her a fifty-dollar bill. '*Grazie.*'

Already the members of the orchestra were looking to him for guidance. He stood, murmuring, 'I have to go.'

Carly sat at the table with shockwaves rattling her composure. Here she was trying to avoid his advances, and he'd already locked her out. A small ache swelled inside her, along with the feeling she'd missed something just short of paradise.

'Would you like something, signorina?' The waitress stood before her with a pad and pencil in hand.

Carly shook her head. The only thing she needed now was a level head to play that aria the way it was meant to be played. Michelangelo had distracted her enough.

* * *

Carly spent Tuesday in a never-ending slew of rehearsals for their last concert at the Arch of Peace. Michelangelo made no move to speak with her, which was fine with her, because the aria had never sounded better. This time she'd get it right.

The audience at the Arch of Peace was absurdly large, covering the entire rounded square of the Piazza Sempione and spilling into the main city park. People brought lawn chairs and blankets, and some even sat on the grass, reminding Carly of the fourth of July fireworks show at the Hatch Memorial Shell along the Charles River in Boston.

Behind them the Arch rose in a colossal stone structure of solidarity and truth. Its origins dated back to the Roman walls of Milan. For Carly, it brought no peace.

Her heart sped as she stood on the makeshift stage Michelangelo had constructed solely for this event. Alaina stretched beside her, closing her eyes to envision her character in the aria. Wolf stood on his podium, his baton raised. Behind him sat the entire orchestra with their instruments ready and waiting to play. This was the moment of truth, their last chance to prove themselves.

She brought her reed to her lips. The song began like all the others, with her chirpy sixteenth notes. Her fingers shook, making the notes feel rushed and edgy when they should have danced with joy. She scanned the audience, which a performer should never do while playing. Michelangelo sat in the front row. Instead of watching her, he gazed down at his feet. His disinterest, or more like feigned ambivalence, sent a shockwave through her gut.

She lost her support, and the reed felt like a closed-off tube in her mouth. Her oboe squawked, and the ugly noise reverberated across the square like a dying duck.

Alaina's eyes widened as she took a breath and came in, stumbling on her words. She reached for a high note, and her voice faltered before she picked up the melody again.

Face burning with embarrassment, Carly kept playing, feeling as if she had been roasted in front of everyone like a pig on a spit. The aria dragged on with Alaina's shaky words and her own disjointed notes until every nerve on her body shook. She ended the final cadence with a sour note that just went flatter at the end.

Silence fell as the audience decided how to react. Carly brought her reed down from her lips as Alaina walked prematurely off stage, leaving her standing there alone. Then, a single person clapped. She glanced down to see Michelangelo rising in a standing ovation. He looked like a fool, but he didn't care. He only had eyes for her. Around him, light applause began as they followed his example.

Carly narrowed her gaze and looked away. It was too little too late. She'd allowed him to get too close to her emotions, and in doing so, he'd ruined their aria and her last chance to prove herself on the tour. In that moment, she vowed never to let a man distract her again.

CHAPTER SEVENTEEN

Accent

This time it didn't take a musical genius to know that something had gone terribly wrong in the aria. While Carly struggled with the music, Michelangelo felt as though he was right up there with her. Every ounce of heartbreak, embarrassment, and shame spread directly to him.

It was all his fault.

He'd distracted her this whole tour by leading her on, then cutting her off as though she was nothing to him. But she was so much more.

Carly was the first woman that had made him forget about his problems with the winery. She proved to him he could have a life outside the vineyard, and she made him feel youthful and sexy again when so many of his family's problems rested on his shoulders. He loved her dry sense of humor and her blunt honesty.

And now he'd lost her.

As Carly's eyes narrowed at him, he died a little inside. He could hardly blame her; he'd been an *idiota* earlier on in the day.

The concert ended, and Michelangelo shot up from his seat to find her. He had no idea what he'd say, but he had to try. It wasn't every day a woman like that came around, and he couldn't let her go that easily. But where would she go after such an embarrassing spectacle?

Backstage. Of course.

As he walked around the stage, Ms. Maxhammer's voice stopped him in his tracks. 'Another wonderful evening, Mr. Ricci.'

He turned around and gave her his most sincere smile. 'I do my best.'

Her gray curls had been reformed into a glossy wave. She looked like old Hollywood royalty. 'What an excellent idea to have this final concert here at such a monumental icon of Milan.'

'I must say the location was purely your maestro's idea. All I did was to make it happen.'

Her fingers touched her neck, where a ruby necklace sparkled in the concert lights. 'And so modest, too.' She grabbed his sleeve and pulled him close. 'Tell me, do you have any faults?'

Faults? Like lying about being an experienced tour guide? Or distracting the lead oboist enough to ruin the last concert? He gulped down his reply. 'Several, I'm afraid. Although such a great evening is not the time to dredge them up.'

She wiggled her finger at him. 'Touché, Mr. Ricci, touché.'

A blur of red over her shoulder caught his eye. Was it Carly?

Michelangelo needed to find her before she got back to the hotel, or she'd never let him into her room. 'If you'll excuse me, I have to—'

Alaina pushed through the crowd, almost blinding him with her bejeweled monstrosity of a dress. She positioned herself between them as if they'd invited her to join the conversation. 'Michelangelo, please excuse me, I have urgent news for Ms. Maxhammer.'

'Of course.' He moved to turn away, but Alaina grabbed his arm. 'And I'd like to speak with you afterward.'

He resisted the urge to recoil. *Splendido. Just what I wanted.* 'I don't mean to intrude if this is a private conversation.'

'It's not, and it won't take long.' She turned to Ms. Maxhammer. 'Carly Davis has disappeared.'

Michelangelo blinked in shock.

Ms. Maxhammer narrowed her eyes. 'What do you mean?'

Alaina smacked her lips together. 'She took off after our aria, and hasn't been seen since. The second oboe played her solos in the last piece.'

Ms. Maxhammer scanned the crowd. 'Well, maybe she got sick. Has anyone called the hotel?'

'I have, ma'am, and no one's in our room. They say she hasn't checked in yet.'

'Well then, where could she be?'

Alaina put both her hands on her hips. 'I think she was so embarrassed that she ruined my aria that she snuck off like a coward.'

Ms. Maxhammer wrinkled her already wrinkled brow. 'She's supposed to attend this evening's reception.'

Alaina's lips twitched as if she held back a smirk. 'I have reason to believe she may have gone out…' she paused for effect. 'Drinking.'

'Ha!' Ms. Maxhammer scoffed. 'Drinking on the job?'

Michelangelo placed his hand on her arm. 'You don't know that. She probably had some sort of emergency.' Then an idea brightened in his mind, he could save Carly, give him a chance to talk with her, and get him away from Alaina all at the same time. 'Let me go look for her.'

Alaina gaped as though he'd pulled some trick on her. 'Picking up drunk orchestra members is not in your job description.'

He ignored her and looked to Ms. Maxhammer. 'I found Trixie, and I can find her.'

'Very well.' Ms. Maxhammer waved him away. 'Go find her before she gets into trouble. The streets of Milan are like any other big city. It's not a place where you want to get lost, especially if you're not in your right mind.'

'Yes, ma'am.' Michelangelo moved, but a vice-like grip closed on his arm. He turned around, knowing full well who to expect.

Alaina stared at him like a jealous girlfriend. 'I'm coming with you.'

He pried her fingers off. 'No you're not. You have to stay with the orchestra and greet the audience in the reception, as per Ms. Maxhammer's wishes.'

She put hands on her curvy hips. 'I'm not under the same contract as the rest of the orchestra, I'm a soloist.'

'Very well, but I don't need your help. I'll find her faster if I go alone.'

Her lower lip trembled. 'What about us?'

He swallowed her comment hard. 'Us?'

'You know there's only two more days of the tour, and you haven't even come over to say a word to me. If you think you can just go kissing me that first night, and then—'

'Listen.' He took her arm and brought her over to a quiet place. 'You forced that kiss. All I've been is cordial to you, like everyone else in this orchestra. It's my job. But as for *us*, there is no *us*.' At this point he didn't care if she complained and he lost his job. The charade could go on no longer.

Alaina put her hand up to her neck and stifled a quiet little sob. 'You don't mean that.'

Michelangelo leaned in, giving her his most serious glare. 'I do.'

'Damn it.' She stomped on the cobblestone. 'Every guy I meet is Mr. Wrong. I'm never going to fall in love.'

As much as he felt bad for her, he couldn't be the one to show her love. He had feelings for someone else, someone who'd gone missing, maybe put herself in danger. He turned and pushed through the crowd before Alaina could stop him. She'd already done enough.

He jumped into his Fiat and merged into traffic before he realized he had absolutely no idea where Carly would go. He pulled over, took out his phone and tried her number. He was sent directly to voicemail.

Merda! He put both hands on the wheel and placed his forehead on the rim. This was all his fault. If he hadn't led her on in the first place—after all, what with his winery problems, he knew things couldn't have gone anywhere between them—then she would have never bombed the aria and jeopardized her career—the one thing that meant the most to her. He'd been such an *idiota,* and he had to make things right. *Where would she go?*

The only other place she knew of in Milan was the Galleria. Flinging on his turn signal, he maneuvered back into the traffic, weaving between the larger trucks.

Lit by the golden storefront lights, the Galleria was even more magical at night. Michelangelo jogged the length of the storefronts. Most of the shops had closed, leaving only the restaurants and bars, overfilling with patrons with queues curving around the front.

In all of Milan, did he really think she'd come back here? It was the only place she knew of. Carly was a practical woman. She wouldn't take chances with a place she didn't know—even if she was out of her mind.

He walked in circles, until he found himself on top of the bull mosaic in the center. He'd never believed in the tradition of spinning on the bull—just another way to get tourists into the Galleria to shop. But, desperate to find her, he closed his eyes and spun on his heels.

The force of his spin whipped through his hair. He'd cast himself adrift. His vinery was slipping through his fingers, his mother lost more of her memories every day, and now he'd met the most amazing woman only to drive her away.

Please, let me find her.

When he stopped, his gaze settled on Zucca's Bar, the place with the longest wait. That's where he'd try. Getting in line, he smoothed his suit and hair and put on his most charming smile. The hostess was a young woman in her early twenties, with her silken black hair pulled up into a high ponytail.

He placed both his hands on her hostess stand and spoke in a low velvety voice. '*Buona sera, signorina.*'

She giggled. '*Buona sera, signore.* Would you like me to take your name for this list?'

'No, thank you. I'm meeting someone here.'

She pouted. 'A woman?'

'Yes, an American woman by the name of Carly Davis.'

She checked the list, chewing on the end of her pen. 'I don't see her name here, signore.'

He considered turning away. Was he really going to listen to a mosaic of a bull? Still, he had to be thorough if he was ever to find her. 'She may have gone straight to the bar. Please allow me to check inside.'

She shook her pen at him playfully. 'You cannot cut the line, signore.'

He smiled, catching her eyes. He took her hand with the pen and lowered it to the hostess stand. 'I assure you, she saved a seat. If I'm wrong, I'll find my way out.'

She watched his hand on hers. 'Can I trust you, signore?'

He winked. 'Certemente.'

She gave him a sideways smile. 'Go on, the bar's in the back.'

Maybe he still had some of that smooth as gelato charm? If so, he was going to need it.

Michelangelo breathed with relief as he cut through the tables and circled around waiters and waitresses with steaming dishes and glasses of wine.

He turned into a smaller antechamber in the back, where people sat at a circular bar watching television and flirting over martinis. A few private booths sat in the back.

No Carly.

Disappointment rushed up, and he squelched it down. Really, did he expect to find her in the very first place he looked? Life just wasn't that easy. At least not for him, not these days.

A flash of red caught his attention from the back booth. The waiter brought over a tray with a strawberry margarita, and a slender arm wearing the same dress Carly had worn on stage snaked out. The waiter spoke in Italian, and she spoke in perfect Italian back, with a slight accent he'd tried to teach her how to erase.

Carly was here.

Now, he had to figure out how to convince her to give him a second chance.

CHAPTER EIGHTEEN

One More

Carly told the waiter to keep them coming in Italian. She licked the salt off the rim and sipped her margarita, the cool tanginess calming her parched throat. *Two more days.*

In two days she could jump right back on that plane and pick up her life where she'd left it in Boston. No more Italy, no more arias, no more Michelangelo. Sure she had to get back to the orchestra and finish the tour—all they had left were personal vacation days anyway. But two or three more margaritas wouldn't hurt.

When she'd told Michelangelo in the bus that first day she'd never be coming back, she meant it. The entire country was a tease, right down to its snarky reviewers and hot-and-cold tour guide.

'Is this seat taken, signorina?'

In her second margarita buzz, it took her a moment to recognize the voice. She turned her head slowly, dreading the one person she didn't want to see again. What the hell was he doing here?

'It is.'

He crossed his arms. 'Looks empty to me.'

She leveled with him. It was all she could do. 'What are you doing here?'

Michelangelo slipped into the booth across from her. 'Ms. Maxhammer's looking for you. Thanks to Alaina, she knows you're out drinking.'

'Alaina. Yes, let's talk about her.' Carly took a large sip and stared him down. 'One girlfriend isn't enough for you?'

'I told you. She was never my girlfriend, and tonight I told her so. She won't be a problem anymore.'

Carly wiped her mouth on her napkin. 'You did it because the tour is ending. Cut me off, then cut her off like some game.'

His stared intensely. 'No, I did it for you.'

Carly stopped mid sip. 'For me?' Her words came out sarcastically. The alcohol had stripped her normal politeness filter, but she didn't care.

'Alaina wanted to come with me to look for you, but I wanted to find you myself, so we could talk.'

Carly waved her hand as if swatting a fly—a Michelangelo fly. 'Talk about what?'

'About what I've been keeping from you this entire trip.'

That got her attention. She pushed her margarita away. 'And what's that?' A wife at home? She wouldn't be surprised.

He sighed and placed both arms on the table. Sheer vulnerability shone through his eyes. 'I'm not a tour guide. In fact, the only tours I ever gave were on my family's vineyard as a kid. *Cavolo*, I'm more interested in pruning grapevines and fermenting the perfect robust wine than remembering when St. Peter's Basilica was built.'

His words sobered her and she dropped the sarcastic façade. 'So what are you doing here?'

'My winery has had a few rough years since my father passed away. We had some droughts and problems with pests. We're no longer able to pay the mortgage my father signed when he refinanced our land for more fields. My landlords are breathing down my throat. They already set up a new lease with someone who's going to tear the whole place down. That's why I had to leave the banquet the other night—to buy my winery more time.'

Her margarita turned to acid in her stomach. 'That's horrible.'

He rubbed his forehead. 'And that's not all. My mother has Alzheimer's. She's slipping away more and more every day, and the winery is the only thing that brings back her memories. If I take her away, she'll spiral downhill quickly. I will have lost both my parents and everything they worked for.'

The reality of his situation tore her apart. He was no longer an Italian playboy, but a hardworking family man trying his best to keep his life together. No wonder he cut it off between them. He had greater problems to deal with. 'Why didn't you tell me before?'

He shook his head. 'I didn't know if I could trust you. You could have gone straight to Ms. Maxhammer and told her the truth. And you wouldn't have been acting wrongly. She deserves that. Everyone on the tour deserves it.'

Carly reached across the table and grabbed both his hands. 'Nonsense. You've been doing a fabulous job. Aside from annoying Reena, which isn't the end of the world, you've shown the orchestra a grand time. They all love you. Why would I jeopardize that?'

'So you forgive me?'

All the walls she'd built around her came crashing down. His honesty and his vulnerability drew her to him more now than ever. She squeezed his hands. 'Of course I do. Your secret is safe with me.'

He threaded his fingers through hers, pulling her closer across the table. 'Then I have one more confession to make.'

The dizziness of the buzz cleared into a heightened sense of clarity. Her heart thudded heavily in her chest. 'Yes?'

'From the moment I laid eyes on you, I knew you were special. We had an electric connection from that first trip on the bus. From there, it only grew until neither of us could ignore it. I told you before that now is not the right time to get involved. But what we have is too special, too wonderful to throw away. I was wrong.'

He unthreaded his hand and rose. At first she thought he was leaving her before things got out of hand, but instead, he slipped into the booth beside her. 'I would never forgive myself if I let you go so easily.'

His proximity intoxicated her more than any slew of margaritas. She put both hands on his chest, feeling the hard ridges of
his lean muscles and the strong beat of his heart. He rubbed his
cheek against hers, the rough stubble igniting her skin. Her lips
moved to his, and he pulled her into his arms. She opened her
mouth, and the kiss deepened, causing a burning sensation deep
within her gut.

Carly had never been kissed like that before. The raw passion
awakened something long-dormant inside of her, a primal urge
stronger than any of her music. All she wanted was his closeness,
his caresses.

Glass shattered from the booth beside them and Michelangelo
pulled back.

Alaina stood from the booth, her fingers shaking. Tears streaked
her face, running a spidery web of mascara down each cheek. A
piece of broken glass stuck from her palm, leaking blood on her
red dress. She must have shattered her wine glass in her hands.
'She may not tell Ms. Maxhammer about your lies, but I will.'

Michelangelo stood. 'Alaina. I can explain.'

'You don't need to.' Alaina's glance shot at Carly. 'And you!
You said you weren't interested in him. You lied to me as well. I
thought you were my friend.'

Guilt hit Carly like a slap in the face. Alaina thought of her
as a friend? Sure, they'd spent a lot of time rehearsing, but had
she really made that big an impression on her? Then, the truth
dawned on her—Alaina probably didn't have that many friends,
so any gesture Carly had made would have been enough for her
to think of her as one.

Then, she remembered Michelangelo's words. Vehemence boiled
inside her. 'What kind of friend sells you out to the boss when
you disappear for one night?'

Alaina glanced down as though Carly was the one who'd hurt
her more. 'I was angry with how the aria came off, and I went

163

to find you, and you weren't there. You'd abandoned me to face all those people alone.' She stopped in mid-sentence, clutching her stomach. Carly froze. She *had* abandoned Alaina. Whether she liked it or not, they had become friends, and not only had Carly left her after the aria, she'd stolen her supposed boyfriend as well. 'I'm sorry.'

'It's too late for Sorry.' Alaina pulled away as tears overcame her.

Carly sat in shock, watching Alaina run from the bar. What had she done? It was over. They'd been caught: she was drinking when she should have been mingling at the event after the concert, and Michelangelo was cavorting with the customers. Worse, yet, she'd just betrayed one of the orchestra's greatest benefactors. Alaina knew Michelangelo's secret, and soon he'd have no job. To be so close to nirvana, then to have it ripped away was more painful than anything Carly had ever experienced in her life. Yet, she wasn't alone, and that small comfort gave her courage. They'd face this together.

She took Michelangelo's hand. 'She's right. I did betray her.'

'Nonsense.' If it wasn't clear before, it was clear now. Michelangelo had no feelings for Alaina, no remorse. 'What she did, she did to herself.'

His unforgiving attitude surprised her. 'What do you mean?'

'She forced herself on me back there in the hotel room, and then every day after that. I had to be polite because of my job, but she misinterpreted every single word I said.'

Carly couldn't believe she was standing up for her, but she did. 'Alaina only did it because she's looking for love.'

Michelangelo shook his head as though Alaina finding love was a hopeless endeavor. 'Well, she's looking in the wrong place.'

'Wrong place or not, she's pretty angry.' Carly sighed. 'What should we do?'

He plopped down in his seat already giving in to defeat. 'We can't stop her.'

'Yes, but we can explain our side.' She nudged him from the

booth. An hour ago, she'd been too ashamed to confront anyone in the orchestra, and now she'd walk in front of every one of them, right up to Ms. Maxhammer for him and make things right again. 'Come on. Take me back to the reception.'

They left the Galleria in Michelangelo's Fiat, weaving through the other cars on the street.

Carly held onto the door while Michelangelo sped through the yellow light. 'Do you think we can get to her before Alaina does?'

He shrugged. 'That depends on which cab she took and how much she was willing to pay him.'

Alaina could buy the entire orchestra if she wanted. 'Then that doesn't bode well for us.'

They reached the Piazza Del Milan, the grand hotel built in the ancient Roman fashion, where the reception was taking place. While Carly jumped out and grabbed her purse and oboe bag, Michelangelo left the car with the valet. 'Where is the Ballroom Giardino?'

The valet took the keys. 'Second floor, third door to your right, signore.' Carly wanted to ask him if he'd seen another red-dressed woman parading in, but that would only waste time.

'*Grazie.*' Michelangelo took Carly's hand. Carly held her dress up in a clump of sparkly fabric and they ran to the elevators.

Elegant chamber music greeted them as the doors closed, mocking their situation. Carly gripped Michelangelo's hand, wanting to continue that tease of a kiss in the booth. But now was not the time. The doors parted and they walked into the ballroom. Orchestra members danced on an oak floor while a jazz band played *What a Wonderful World*. Wolf and Melody sat at a long white-clothed table eating trays of fruits and cheese, and Al flirted with a waitress. No one seemed to notice them.

'Where's Ms. Maxhammer?' Carly scanned the room.

'I'm over here.' The old woman's icy voice chilled Carly's heart. Carly nudged Michelangelo's arm and they turned toward the hallway beside the room.

Ms. Maxhammer stood with one hand on her hip and her other hand on her cane. 'And I hear you have quite the story to tell.'

Carly's stomach flipped. Alaina had already reached her. Was it too late? Michelangelo squeezed Carly's hand, giving her courage. 'Where's Alaina? Is she all right?'

Ms. Maxhammer nodded. 'She's fine. I sent her to her room with my nurse.'

'So she told you what she saw?' Carly could barely keep her beating heart in her chest.

'She told me everything…from her point of view.' Ms. Maxhammer gestured over her shoulder. 'Come. Let's talk where there's more privacy.'

They walked to a private conference room with paintings of the green countryside and wineries that must have resembled Michelangelo's own home. Ms. Maxhammer took a seat at the head of a circular oak table, settling into the leather conference chair. Carly and Michelangelo sat on either side. Carly couldn't help feeling as though she was in the principal's office for skipping class.

Ms. Maxhammer breathed deeply and turned to Michelangelo. 'Alaina's disputes are mostly with you. She's told me you're not the experienced tour guide you said you are, and that you are a lady's man going after all the pretty young women on this trip.'

Carly wanted to defend him, but it wasn't her place, so she sat back and let him talk.

'My apologies for deceiving you.' Michelangelo bowed his head. 'I took the job because I needed the money to save my winery.'

The old woman pursed her lips. 'So I deduced.'

Michelangelo spread his hands upon the table. 'But I'm not a ladies' man. Actually, far from it. I've spent every waking minute of my life trying to save my winery. If that meant being cordial to the orchestra members, then that's what I did. I was never involved with Alaina. She projected her feelings onto me. I tried to tell her so tonight, and I realized it was too late. I should have said something during the tour, but I didn't want to upset her.'

A hint of a smile crept into Ms. Maxhammer's lips. 'That's quite believable, knowing her.'

Michelangelo took Carly's hand, surprising her. 'The last thing I thought I'd have on this tour was feelings for someone.' He shook his head. 'God knows, I have enough problems of my own, and romance would only make my life more complicated. But, no matter how much I fight them, I do have feelings for Carly. Whether or not I lose this job, what I feel toward her will remain.'

'I see.' The old woman turned to Carly with a sparkle in her eye. 'And what say you on this matter?'

Carly shrugged, feeling sheepish. Her feelings for Michelangelo eclipsed anything she had with the orchestra. If she went down in flames, then so be it. At least she'd have given herself a chance at romance. 'I have feelings for him, too. I want his winery to succeed. He's really done nothing wrong. All he's ever done this whole trip was show us a good time. We should allow him to continue as tour guide and pay him for the time he's spent providing us with a wonderful tour.'

Ms. Maxhammer tapped her fingernails on the table. 'Michelangelo has done a magnificent job on this tour, whether he had experience or not. Yet we have a very unhappy customer, someone who's donated a lot of money to this tour, and she has some valid arguments up her sleeve.'

Carly crossed her arms. So that's how Alaina got that solo. Why did they always have to pander to the rich? Why couldn't they choose the best woman for the part?

Ms. Maxhammer spread her hands out as if she were helpless. 'If Alaina's not happy by the morning, she'll take this up with the rest of the board, and with Wolf. What do you suggest I do?'

Just when she thought she'd found the missing piece, Carly's world was falling apart. Michelangelo would lose his winery, she'd go home with a nasty slew of reviews, and everyone in the orchestra would think she was the biggest flirt ever. She'd never be able to show her face again and she'd end her relationship

167

with Michelangelo on a sour note—no pun intended. If only she had more time.

Then a crazy idea brightened in Carly's mind. She reached across the table and grabbed Ms. Maxhammer's hand. 'Propose one more concert. The orchestra is here for another two days anyway. And they all love Michelangelo. Why not give a performance on Michelangelo's vineyard to raise money for his cause? Not only would it help him, but it would give Alaina and I another chance at that aria and a good review. That's what she truly wants.'

Michelangelo waved her idea away. 'No, I won't have it. Too many people have to make a sacrifice for me.'

Carly patted the back of his hand. 'It's not just for you, it's also to set things right with Alaina. Give her one more chance to impress with her aria and she'll forgive you.'

Ms. Maxhammer tilted her head. 'That, young lady, is the best idea I've heard all night.' She rose from her seat and Michelangelo helped her up. 'I'll ask them now. But I have to warn you, everyone in the orchestra has to agree to it. This was supposed to be their time off.'

He helped her to the door. 'They probably all want to go to the beach at this point. Not fundraise for me.'

'No.' Carly bolted ahead and opened the door, finally feeling a sense of exhilarating relief. 'Americans are fiercely loyal. You're wrong.'

CHAPTER NINETEEN

A Favor to Ask

Michelangelo's stomach clenched as he stood before all of the orchestra members. He'd cursed these people at the beginning, thinking them lazy, rude Americans. Now when he gazed down at Bertha's mischievous wink, at Trixie's awkward wave, and at Carly's loving sincerity, he knew they had a special place in his heart. Guilt mixed with melancholy trickled through him. He hated asking them for help during their time off, but the fate of his winery now rested on their shoulders.

Ms. Maxhammer took the stage and turned on the mic. 'At the grand conclusion of this wonderful tour, I must ask you one more favor. Listen carefully, for you will have to give up your remaining days in Italy to make this happen, and none of you are under contract to do so. These are your days off to spend as you will.' She paused, letting the moment sink in. The room grew so silent he could have heard a cell phone vibrate in someone's pocket.

Ms. Maxhammer knew how to create anticipation. She tapped her fingers on the podium, then continued. 'It has come to my attention that our wonderful tour guide, Michelangelo, needs our help.'

'Anything we can do.' Bertha waved her hand. 'He can stay with me if he needs a room.' Her friend Trudy covered her mouth.

Ms. Maxhammer raised a hand to silence the growing murmurs. 'It's nothing like that. At least not yet.' She pursed her lips. 'Turns out he's not an experienced tour guide.'

Hushed mumbles and a few grunts of disapproval surrounded them.

'I knew it!' Reena pointed at him. 'I knew that "Brotherhood of the Manifesto" was crap.'

Michelangelo winced. Maybe he had gone a little overboard.

Mrs. Maxhammer raised her hand. 'We're not here to hang him, we're here to help him. He's done a wonderful job as our tour guide, and I want you to take that into account.'

A few people nodded in agreement.

Mrs. Maxhammer touched the gaudy pearls at her neck. 'He took this job because his winery—one that has been in his family for generations—is in danger.'

Gasps rang out, followed by more mutterings. Trixie pushed through the crowd. 'Ms. Maxhammer, how can we help?'

'He needs to raise money to purchase the land, or it will be leveled and made into condos.'

'No way.' Trixie twisted her hair around her finger.

'Why didn't he tell us?' Al shouted out from the back.

Ms. Maxhammer pursed her lips and gave Michelangelo a knowing look. 'He didn't want to burden you with his problems.' She gestured toward Carly. 'Carly Davis has proposed a magnificent idea to help him and give her and Alaina another chance at their aria. But it would take all of you to agree to make it happen.'

'What is it?' Bertha chewed her lower lip.

Ms. Maxhammer spread her hands like a magic trick. 'A benefit concert at Michelangelo's vineyard Thursday night. Proceeds will go to the restoration of his property and the lease.'

Murmurs echoed throughout the orchestra. Melody spoke in hushed tones with Wolf. Al scratched his head and Trixie's parents whispered excitedly in each other's ears. Embarrassment crept up Michelangelo's neck to his cheeks. These were professional musicians. They hardly ever played for free.

Ms. Maxhammer tapped her finger on the mic, silencing the talking. 'Since I'd have to get into advertising this right away, I must see now, by a show of hands, how many of you would be willing to add yet another concert—a free concert, mind you—to the tour?'

Bertha put her hand up first, followed by Trixie and her parents.

'Well, heck, I'm not going to the beach by myself.' Bertha's friend Trudy came next.

Maestro Braun stood from his table, followed by Carly's bff, Melody. One by one, the entire orchestra joined in.

Even Al raised him hand. 'One more for good time's sake.'

Warmth spread through Michelangelo's chest, followed by guilt and embarrassment. Boy, had he misjudged them.

Al shouted over, 'Does that mean we get a free bottle of wine?'

'Absolutely.' Michelangelo glowed with positive warmth. After all he'd been through this was like a beacon in a dark and scary storm and he had Carly to thank for it. His gaze settled on her as she held her hand up higher than the rest. 'Everyone gets a bottle of wine.'

Ms. Maxhammer touched the mic again. 'Well, now—a unanimous vote. Everything is settled. Tomorrow I'll make the arrangements with the media.' She turned to Carly and Michelangelo and winked. 'You two are free to get over there in the morning and start setting up. I'll handle Alaina.'

'No I'll do it.' Carly interjected with a strong determination that surprised him.

Ms. Maxhammer raised both eyebrows.

Carly's face softened. 'I've broken her trust, and I want to apologize. I want to make things right between us. After all, we have to play together for this plan to succeed. There's no way we're going to produce beautiful music if we hate each other.'

'Very well.' Mrs. Maxhammer nodded as if impressed. 'She's

requested her own room, so you'll have to ask her to come in.'

'Great.' Carly breathed heavily. He admired her for her determination. Only a truly brave woman would stand up to make things right.

Mrs. Maxhammer touched Carly's arm gently. Amusement danced in her eyes. 'Good luck.'

*****

Carly took a deep breath and knocked on the door to Alaina's room. When no one answered, she tried again, this time louder. 'It's Carly. Open the door.'

Silence. This would be harder than she thought. Carly steeled her nerves. 'Alaina, I'm sorry.'

More silence.

'I should have told you from the start I had feelings for Michelangelo, but at first I thought he was with you, so I tried to convince myself I didn't like him.'

Still silent. Was she even in there?

'I have another way for you to get the review you want.'

The door opened. Alaina stared back at her with mascara-smeared eyes. She wore a silky robe—thankfully covering her sleepwear. 'How?'

'I've spoken with Mrs. Maxhammer and planned another concert.'

Alaina shrugged. 'It doesn't matter. The aria has never sounded good. It will just be another embarrassment.'

The fact that she came to answer the door gave Carly hope. 'You don't know that.'

She leaned on the doorway. At least she wasn't slamming the door in her face. 'What makes you think this will be any different?'

'It will be different if you want it to be different.' Carly stepped toward her and lowered her voice. 'We've had this weird situation with Michelangelo between us and it's affected the way we've played together.'

'I'll say.' She snorted.

Frustration bristled the hairs on Carly's neck. Getting Alaina to forgive her was like climbing an unscaleable mountain. She ran her hands through her hair. 'If we can forgive each other, then we'll play better together.'

Alaina shrugged, glancing at her as though she was the enemy. 'What are you going to steal next? My dress?'

'No, you can have that.' Carly smiled. *Get to the truth of the matter.* 'I hadn't realized we'd become friends. But, when I saw the hurt in your face, I felt guilty—like I'd betrayed someone close to me—a *friend*. We've spent a lot of time together, and I know it's been hard at times. We're not exactly two peas in a pod.'

A small smile worked its way onto Alaina's lips. 'No, we're not.'

'But, we've learned to get along together, and I think we can learn to play together as well. You want to return to America with a favorable review don't you?'

Alaina nodded. 'It's why I came on this trip. My career's been stagnant for a long time and I need something to propel it forward.'

Carly knew about career all too well. 'That I can understand.' She reached over and touched Alaina's arm. 'I want that for you, too. I want to make things right between us, if you'll let me.'

Alaina nodded slowly. 'Maybe I don't need love right now. Maybe all I need is a friend.'

Carly sniffed back her own tears. 'That's what I need, too.'

*****

Apprehension hung over Carly as she and Michelangelo sped down the rain-slicked highway in his red Fiat. She owed it to Mrs. Maxhammer, Alaina, the rest of the orchestra, and to him to make sure this concert was a success. 'Something bothering you?' He glanced at her from the driver's side.

She folded and unfolded her hands in her lap. 'It's just that we have less than twenty-four hours to put on a successful event on a massive scale. What if no one comes?'

'Then, you've done your best to save something that can't be saved.' Michelangelo gave her a warm smile, albeit sad. 'I appreciate everything you and your orchestra are doing for me.'

'It's the least I can do.' Too caught up in her own gig world, Carly had never really helped anyone with any cause before. It felt so good to be able to support someone else, someone she had growing feelings for. Those feelings felt blissful as well. She had no idea where they'd go, but right now she wanted to experience every moment with Michelangelo that she could. It seemed like their moments together were just as numbered as the ones the winery had.

They sped across the rolling hills outside Milan onto a windy, overgrown driveway. Carly had enough of an imagination to see what the drive could look like once the hedges were trimmed back and the sidewalks repaired. Beautiful mosaics of people enjoying wine in the countryside lined the walls, illuminated in the morning sunlight.

They crested a ridge and the rows of vines came into view. Carly gasped. 'It's gorgeous.' Normally, she wasn't one to notice landscapes, but Michelangelo's story had gripped her heart. This land had belonged to his ancestors, his parents, and now him.

Michelangelo winked. 'You've seen nothing yet.'

They wove through the vineyard to a large estate made from beige stucco, red brick, and stone. It reminded her of the mansion in the Godfather movie, with a fountain in the center of a circular drive. Despite being ostentatious and bucolic, there was a timeless-ness and homey quality to the grounds. An easy, relaxed vibe came over her; she felt she could vacation here for a very, very long time.

'This is all yours?'

'Until the end of the week, yes.' Michelangelo parked the car and looked over at her. 'It's nice to see you here, like I'm bringing home the last piece of the puzzle.'

Excitement swelled up inside her. What exactly did he mean by that? Not willing to confront that topic just yet, she covered the serious nature of the conversation with a joke. 'Hopefully, you'll be bringing home much more than that.'

He laughed and turned off the ignition. 'You're right. Come, let's tell my secretary, Isabella, the bad news.'

'The bad news?' Did he have one more lady up his sleeve? 'You mean the good news, right?'

He laughed. 'Watch her face when she realizes just how many people are coming.'

'Oh.' Relieved, Carly opened her door and stepped out. The fresh air of the countryside washed over her. She span around in the drive, feeling as though she had walked into a fairytale. Michelangelo had grown up here, so this place was an integral part of him. Getting to know the winery was like discovering a whole new side of him, a side that drew her further in.

They walked to the office beside the main building. 'You sure she'll be working this early in the morning?'

'Knowing Isabella, she'll come in at dawn to make sure the last crates are packaged and ready to go for today's deliveries.'

'That's dedication.'

Michelangelo showed her to the door. 'Her whole family has lived on the vineyard for generations, and her husband works in the fields, so any investment she makes is in her own family's future.'

'I see.' Carly hadn't thought of all the other people who depended on this winery. Heck, it must employ hundreds of people. Saving the winery meant saving their jobs as well.

Carly walked into an overstuffed office, filled with crates of wine, piles of paperwork and filing cabinets. A woman so pregnant Carly worried she'd have the baby right then sat behind a desk, illuminated by the fluorescent glow of a computer screen. She gazed up from her work and a smile stretched across her face. 'Michelangelo.'

'Isabella.' Michelangelo gestured to Carly. 'I'd like you to meet

Carly Davis.'

Isabella rose while holding her belly. She gave Carly an interesting look of appraisal and smiled even wider. 'Signorina.'

'Nice to meet you.'

Michelangelo took Isabella's arm to steady her. Carly guessed
she was going to need it. 'Carly's here to help us save the winery.'

Isabella placed her hand on her heart. 'Mio Dio! You don't say.'

He nodded. 'She's invited her whole orchestra to give a benefit
concert here…Thursday night.'

Isabella froze and panic widened her gaze. 'This Thursday night?
That's in a little over twenty-four hours!'

Michelangelo found her purse. 'I know. That's why we're here.
We're going to help as much as we can. But you, young lady,
should stay right here.'

She settled back into her computer seat. 'Fine. But, if this thing's
tomorrow night, you're going to need all the help you can get.
Rodolfo will be here any minute to start work in the fields. He
can help you get set up.'

Michelangelo rubbed his chin. 'We'll have to bring out all of
the plastic chairs we used for your wedding, along with the event
tent out back in the barn.'

Isabella's fingers flew over the keyboard. 'I'll send an e-mail to
the team. They can start setting up right away.'

'Setting up for what?' A wispy, age-wizened voice called from
the back of the room.

Carly whirled around.

A ghostly woman leaned on the doorframe, a pink nightgown
clinging to her bony frame. Her hair rose in gray wisps on her
head, and she had Michelangelo's dark, deep-set amber-blue eyes.
Compassion swirled through Carly as she remembered what he'd
told her of his mother's Alzheimer's. To hear it was one thing, but
to see the beautiful woman who'd raised him reduced to a waif
of a memory sent empathy straight to her heart.

Michelangelo ran to her side, hoisting her up. 'Mamma, I'd like you to meet someone very special to me. This is Carly.'

CHAPTER TWENTY

Duets

Carly approached her slowly, holding out her hand. Michelangelo trusted her, and she wanted this moment to be special and not awkward. '*É un piacere conoscerla, signora.*'

The old woman took her hand and turned it over as if she didn't know what to do with it. 'Carly?'

Carly smiled. 'That's right.'

His mother glanced up at him with a keen look. 'A fine wife for you, Michelangelo.'

Wife! Carly blushed as his mother released her hand.

Michelangelo rolled his eyes. 'Mamma, Carly's here with her orchestra. They are coming to play for us.'

She glanced back at Carly, and for a second, the shrewd woman who'd run a winery for decades came back. 'You play an instrument?'

'Yes, I play the oboe.' Hopefully, she knew what that was. Whenever Carly told anyone about the oboe, they always looked confused—as though they weren't sure if it was the black spindly one, or the big long tube.

Michelangelo's mother patted him on the arm. 'You know,

Michelangelo plays the guitar.'

Michelangelo—a musician? Carly gave him a suspicious look. 'You never told me that!'

He laughed and shook his head. 'Very badly.'

The old woman reached out to Carly and took her hand. 'Play for me. Play with Michelangelo. I want to hear a song.'

Michelangelo turned her back to the corridor. 'Mamma, Carly is a professional, classical musician. She doesn't play oldies.' He glanced back to Carly and spoke under his breath, 'Sometimes when I play songs from her past, she remembers things. But you don't have to play today. We have a lot to prepare for.'

'No.' Carly grabbed his arm. 'We can spare a few minutes. Teach me a song and we'll play it for her. I'm a fast learner.'

He sighed, checking the clock on the wall. 'Oh all right. But I can't assure you my guitar is in tune.'

Half the orchestra wasn't in tune. 'That's okay. I'm used to adjusting.'

Carly retrieved her oboe from the car. They walked his mother up to her room, where his mother's nurse profusely apologized. Michelangelo waved her back and gave her the next half hour off. He set up two chairs in front of his mother's bed and dug out his dusty, acoustic guitar. His mother lay under the sheets, tapping her fingers on her stomach in anticipation.

'Play the first verse and I'll listen.' Carly soaked her reed in her *I Love New York* shot glass by her feet.

Michelangelo leaned over his guitar. 'This is a *saltarello*, a traditional Italian folk dance. My mother requested this at her wedding, and later we'd sing it when we danced together when I was a kid.' He took a deep breath. 'The chord structure is a simple one-five-one, going from E-flat major to B-flat.'

'Sounds easy enough.' Carly stuck her reed in. 'I'm ready.'

His fingers paused over the strings.

'What's the matter?'

He laughed. 'I'm nervous.'

A surge of adrenaline hit her. She'd played in front of audiences of thousands. How could she be nervous now? 'I'm nervous, too.'

'You? Nervous?'

'Well, my last performance wasn't so hot.' But it wasn't about that, really. She wanted to impress Michelangelo's mother. She wanted her stamp of approval.

He smiled. 'I don't think that was your fault.'

Before she could respond, he strummed a chord. His fingers plucked a simple, charming melody. After the introduction, he took a deep breath and sang. His bass voice wasn't operatic material, but to Carly it was beautiful with its raw honesty. The words were in Italian, and she could pick out certain phrases about celebrating and love.

When the verse ended, she picked up her oboe and came in, playing in a counter-melody to his vocals. She played at a mezzo forte so as to not cover his voice. Their harmony together struck her as natural and intimate. She could predict his rubatos and speed and slow the music to his pacing along with the melody.

His mother moved her hands through the air as if she were conducting them, lilting back and forth to their beat. She hummed along to their melody, a sparkle dancing in her eyes.

It was the most satisfying musical experience in Carly's life. Playing here with Michelangelo and trying to give a woman back a moment of her precious memories was so much more meaningful than playing for anonymous audiences and critics. This was what music was meant to be, and this was where she was meant to be—alongside Michelangelo at his winery, helping him take care of his ailing mother. A deep ache resonated inside her along with the music. She hadn't felt this way about performing in a long time. The music had stopped becoming a pleasure and had turned into a routine, a job. She'd lost the heart that made it magical. No wonder the critics didn't like her aria.

If only I could stay.

Michelangelo ended the song in a flourish of chords, and Carly tapered the last note to perfection. He brought his guitar down, awestruck and breathless. 'That was wonderful.'

Warm tingles ran all over her, setting her on fire. 'We play together as if we've played together our whole lives.'

He stared into her eyes with a passion she'd never seen before. His lips parted slightly, and she ached to close the distance and kiss them.

His mother clapped. 'Bravo! Bravo!'

Michelangelo set his guitar against the chair and ran to her bedside. He took her hand. 'Did you enjoy it?'

She patted his hand. 'Almost as much as when your father spun me around the dance floor on our wedding day.'

Signora Ricci remembered.

Michelangelo glanced at Carly. His face beamed with joy, melting Carly's heart. He mouthed the words *thank you.*

She should have thanked him. With one song he'd taught her what all of her teachers at the university had only been able to tell her: music could be magical when best shared with those you love.

Michelangelo led Carly from his mother's room, allowing Lila to take over. His mother slept soundly, tucked in the same bed she'd shared with his father for the last fifty years. Michelangelo's great grandfather had carved the headboard with the Ricci arms over a hundred years ago, and it hadn't left the room since. He hoped he could keep it that way.

Michelangelo took Carly's hand, smoothing his thumb over her smooth skin. 'Thank you for what you did back there.'

She glanced down as if shy. 'Thank you for introducing me.'

He'd never seen her like this. Was she really opening up for the first time? Letting down her hard-hitting business face and her witty sarcasm?

Carly squeezed his hand and then let it go. 'What can we do to set up?'

'I can move the chairs and you can tell me where they go.' He smiled. 'Even though I've seen three concerts, I still can't remember how many violins there are.'

Carly laughed. 'I'm not sure I know myself, but I'll try my best.'

He led her outside and they walked to the patio overlooking the vineyard. Rudolfo and the other workers had already transported the stacked chairs from the storage barns out back to the cobblestone.

'Wow, this is where the concert is going to be?' Carly walked to the edge of the cobblestone and blocked her eyes against the sun as it rose in the sky, casting the vineyard in golden light. 'It's magnificent.'

'It's home.' *And it could be hers, too.* The thought hit him hard in the gut. Was he really that serious about her? After less than two weeks? If he'd told himself he'd be falling this hard for an American girl on the tour, he wouldn't have believed it. But now, accepting this tour and meeting her seemed like fate. He'd needed more than money when he took Mrs. Maxhammer's offer. He'd needed someone like Carly. He just hadn't known it yet.

He wanted to put his arm around her and hold her close, watching the sun rise together, but that would be too forward. Carly moved toward the chairs and the moment slipped from his fingers.

'First thing you need to know about an orchestra is that they need space.' Carly took the top chair off the rack and stood it in the center of the patio. 'Or else you'll have a violinists bow poking the piccolo player in the eye.'

'Point taken.' He took the next chair and set it a few feet away. 'How's this?'

'Perfect.' She brought another chair over. 'Make sure they curve out in a semicircle around the conductor's podium.'

'Which is here?' He stood on a patch of broken cobblestone.

Carly smirked. 'No, that's the violas. But you're close.'

'I can see why Mrs. Maxhammer had you go with me.' He ran a hand through his hair. 'If I'd set this up all by myself, you'd have a one-eyed piccolo player and a lost conductor.'

Carly waved her hand. 'You would have been fine. The orchestra can move their chairs around themselves.' She gave him a sly, sideways glance. 'Besides, I don't think setting up is the only reason Mrs. Maxhammer let me come home with you.'

His heart jump-started. 'Oh really? And what is this other reason?'

Carly shrugged and looked away as if she'd said too much. 'Come help me with the next stack. It's too high for me to reach.'

They set up chairs for the rest of the day, making the audience weave in between the rows of vines. Isabella brought them bread and cheese for lunch, but by the end of the day, he was exhausted and ravenous.

Carly had taken off her outer shirt and she looked so sexy in her tank top and shorts. A light sunburn covered her shoulder and the bridge of her nose. 'Is there anything else you can think of that we can do to prepare?'

Michelangelo shook his head. 'I think we've done enough for today. Let's head back to the house.'

Carly wiped sweat from her brow. 'Sounds good to me. My arms feel like they're going to fall off.'

He ran a finger down her arm, wishing he could massage her tired muscles. 'You did a great job. I'm not sure we can fill all the seats you set up.'

'Let's hope so.' Carly walked beside him as they headed toward the house. 'And I didn't do it alone. You set up about twice as many chairs as I did.'

'I'll do anything I can to save this place.' He put his arm around her. 'It feels so good to be able to do something to help my winery. All summer I sat on that patio, watching helplessly as my mother and the vineyard slipped away from me.'

'It must have been awful thinking there was nothing you could do.'

He nodded, relieved he could talk with her about his problems. 'One of those days, Isabella brought me the newspaper. We'd canceled it a long time ago, but I guess that paperboy messed up his route, or forgot. Anyway, that particular paper made it into my hands, and it had Ms. Maxhammer's ad.'

Carly raised an eyebrow. 'Would you call that fate?'

'Perhaps.' Michelangelo tightened his arm around her shoulders, pulling her against him. 'It led me to you.'

Carly felt way too good under his arm, and he didn't think he could hold back any longer. Michelangelo pulled away before he stole a kiss, which would lead to another and another. 'Come, let me make you dinner. You can try some of my family's wine.'

A smile etched its way into the corners of her lips. 'I'd like that very much.'

Michelangelo led her through the back door to the kitchen. A southern-facing window looked out over a patch of old vines from the original vineyard. While Carly watched the moon rise over the hills, he started a pot of boiling water and found a bag of homemade pasta he'd bought at the market down the street. At the time when he bought it, he thought he'd be eating it alone with the jar of homemade tomato sauce, which was just like his mamma used to make. The serendipity of the situation gave him hope.

'The vineyard looks so magical at night.' Carly ran her fingertips along the windowsill. 'You were right when you said there was nothing like it.'

Michelangelo emptied the bag of pasta in the water and warmed the pan of sauce. 'I'm happy to share it with you.'

Carly turned from the window, a flush in her cheeks. Intensity burned in her gaze. 'Being here has brought up emotions inside of me that I didn't think existed.'

Michelangelo's chest tightened. 'Does that scare you?'

Carly laughed. 'Maybe a little. But, more than that, it opens my eyes to a whole new world, a different way of life, more possibilities.' She drew out the word *possibilities* as if inferring a deeper meaning.

The temperature in the kitchen rose fifteen degrees and he didn't think it was the cooking. Michelangelo drained the pasta and stirred in the sauce, thankful to have a task to employ his eager hands. He ached to go over there and wrap his arms around her, but he didn't want to come on too strongly. With his winery on the line, he could be homeless in less than a week. He really couldn't promise her anything. He had nothing to offer. As much as he wanted Carly, he let the comment drift away. 'Dinner is ready.'

Carly walked over. 'Is there something I can help you with?'

Michelangelo pulled out two brightly painted plates from the cupboard. 'Yes.' He gestured toward a wine rack on the countertop. 'Choose a wine.'

As Carly wandered over and pulled out bottle by bottle to read the labels, Michelangelo set the table with two steaming plates of fettuccini. Hopefully, she wasn't one of those carb-counters or a relationship would be almost impossible. Pasta was one of his favorites.

Why I'm thinking about a relationship right now is beyond me. He lit two long tapered candles and the romantic feelings stirring deep inside him came to the surface. He wasn't sure he could hold them down any longer. Part of him didn't care. He'd given everything to this vineyard, so what was one night away from duty?

'How about this one?' She pulled a red Merlot, aged to perfection over the last ten years, from the rack. Those grapes had been harvested by his father when he was still a teen.

Michelangelo smiled. He couldn't have chosen better himself. '*Perfetto!*'

Carly brought the wine to the table, the deep-crimson liquid glowing in the golden candlelight. 'My goodness you've cooked a feast.'

He froze with his hand over the wine-opener. 'You do like pasta, don't you?'

She pulled out her chair and sat down. 'Love it.'

Michelangelo breathed easily. 'Good.'

As he popped the cork and poured two glasses, he wondered just what he was going to do with her. What did she want?

'So, are you enjoying your stay in Italy?'

She sipped her wine and licked her lips, giving him memories of what it tasted like to kiss her. 'I have to say it's grown on me.'

Michelangelo twirled the fettuccini around his fork with practiced grace. 'When I first met you, you said you'd never come back. Is that still true or did I change your mind?'

Carly glanced down at the table, and he couldn't read her expression. 'My life is very complicated, scheduled down to each hour of every day. Being a freelance musician, you have to take every gig offered to you. It's the only way to play the game and win. When I first got here, that's all I could think about—which gigs I was missing out on and how soon I could get back.'

She looked up again, the sheer determination and vulnerability he'd seen in her eyes that first day had come back. 'The funny thing is, right now, I don't want to leave.'

He almost dropped his fork. If only he had his winery, he could offer her a place to stay and explore their feelings for each other, and then, perhaps, establish herself in Italy. But all of that depended on the concert and how much money they raised. Besides, it could just be a passing fancy, and she'd miss her Boston gig life soon enough. The closer he got to her, the more she'd hurt him if she left. This time it would be worse than all the others who'd left before.

'I don't want you to leave, either, but there are some things we may not be able to change.' Michelangelo collected his empty plate and stood still. 'There are guest rooms upstairs. You are welcome to stay in any one of them you'd like.' *As long as this place stands.*

Carly raised an eyebrow. 'Guest rooms?'

'Yes.'

She finished her wine. 'And where will you be sleeping?'

'I have a room down the hall from my mother. It used to be a guest room, but I moved upstairs to keep an eye on her.'

She set the glass down with finality and held his gaze. 'You said I could stay in any one of the guest rooms, right?'

He nodded.

She crossed her legs and leaned back in her chair. 'Well, I'd very much like to see yours.'

Heat rushed from Michelangelo's head to his toes. He'd very much like her to see his room as well. But was this the best for both of them? Right before the big fundraising concert that would decide both their careers? *To hell with it.* He'd handle the aftermath later. 'Shall we?'

CHAPTER TWENTY-ONE

One Night

Carly's heart raced as she followed Michelangelo up the stairs. This was no longer an 'experiment.' Her heart was on the line. Playing duets with him, meeting his mother, and seeing his ailing vineyard had driven her to a place she'd never been before, a crossroads where life took over if she let it. This time she played for keeps.

Michelangelo led her down the corridor past his mother's room. He opened a thick oak door to a smaller, cozier room with embroidered rugs thrown over a stone floor. An ashy fireplace framed with a thick, carved mantel stood across from a four-poster canopy bed draped with sheer fabric. A window looked out to the eastern patch of vines, where the hill slanted into the valley.

Carly felt as though he'd taken her back in time. No cell phones, no televisions or honking cars. Just the two of them and their thoughts in the silence. It was undeniably the most romantic place she'd ever been.

Michelangelo crouched by the fireplace and coaxed a flame from the wood. 'It gets chilly here in the evening toward the end of the summer.'

What chill? Her whole body throbbed with heat. If her neck and cheeks blushed any more, they'd start to steam. But when an Italian hottie invited you into his room and started a fire, you didn't say no.

She walked over to the bed, smoothing the crimson velvet comforter with her fingertips. 'This is your room?'

The fire caught, lighting the room in a golden ambiance. Michelangelo stood, brushing his hands together. 'It is now. As a boy, I used to live downstairs near the kitchen.'

She ran her fingers along the bedpost, carved to resemble roses and vines. A nick in the wood here and there told the tale of ageless years of use. 'So this place has been in your family for generations?'

Michelangelo nodded. 'Since my great, great grandfather.'

The ache she'd felt before returned. How could they tear down such a gorgeous place with so much history? 'I'll do everything I can to keep it in your family, to keep the memories alive.'

'Shhh.' He walked toward her and placed a calloused finger on her lips. 'That's for tomorrow. Right now, we have tonight to ourselves, and I mean to enjoy it.'

A rush of fire trailed up Carly's legs. Electricity buzzed in the air between herself and Michelangelo. He looked dark, brooding and sexy in the mix of shadows and firelight. He leaned down and kissed the top of her head, then moved to her forehead, her cheek, and her lower neck. Each kiss burned her skin and desire stirred within her.

She ran her hands up the lean muscles in his back to his neck, pulling him closer. His lips met hers. She opened her mouth, allowing his tongue to slide across her teeth. Jolts of electricity ran along her nerves. She sighed deeply as he moved her toward the bed. They fell onto the velvet cover, and Carly forgot about her gigs for the first time in her life.

*****

Morning light pierced through Carly's blissful sleep. She turned, burying her head in Michelangelo's bare chest. He smelled like a mix between clean linen and salty man. *Just two more minutes…*

Bangs and thumps, followed by men shouting outside interrupted her peace. What were they doing out there? Then she remembered the e-mail Isabella had sent to the crew to set up for the concert. Carly bolted upright. If tonight didn't go as planned, there'd be no more Italian nights on the vineyard with Michelangelo.

'The concert!'

Michelangelo blinked and rubbed his eyes. 'They're out there already?'

'Yes, and we have to help them.'

He checked his watch. 'Wow, it's nine o'clock already! I never sleep in this late.'

He looked too scrumptious to abandon just yet. She collapsed on top of him and kissed his chest. 'Maybe we tired ourselves out.'

He rolled his eyes as embarrassment softened his gorgeous face. 'I don't want my crew thinking I'm a playboy, bringing home pretty women, or, even worse—a slapper.'

Carly nuzzled against his nose. 'Knowing you and all you've done for this place, I doubt they'd think either.'

She moved away, but Michelangelo pulled her back. 'Wait.'

The gravity of his tone made her heart skip. 'What?'

Intensity flared in his eyes. 'When this is all over, if I still have this winery, I'd like it if you could stay a while—you know, give 'us' a chance.'

There's an 'us?' Carly stopped breathing. This was it—the invitation she'd been waiting for and dreading at the same time. Staying meant leaving her career in Boston behind, but it also meant following her heart. All that waited for her when she got back was work. Here, she had someone who cared about her, someone to build a life with. But restarting a career was a huge undertaking. Even though she'd had some success already, she might never have the same balance of gigs and orchestra that she had in Boston.

The reviews hadn't gotten her off on the best footing. All those years…all that work.

Her phone called to her from across the room, poking out of the front pocket of her purse. She hadn't checked her messages since last night.

Michelangelo stared into her eyes with expectation.

The bright morning light had brought clarity and reality along with it. She sighed. 'Let's take it one step at a time, okay?' Who knew if he'd even have a vineyard? He had enough problems with his mom, and he didn't need one more mouth to feed—which was exactly what he'd have to do until she pieced together a new career here in Italy. Everything was happening too fast and she needed time to think.

Michelangelo's face fell as though she'd stabbed him in the chest. 'Of course.'

Carly pulled away. She couldn't stand to see his disappointment. But she also couldn't give him a promise she might not be able to keep. 'Let's get this show on the road, shall we?' She tried to sound cheerful, but an edge of anxiety worked its way into her words.

They showered, dressed, and ate a quick breakfast. The bus with the musicians pulled up to the front of the estate, and Carly welcomed the orchestra as Michelangelo unloaded the instruments. Bertha and Trudy seemed charmed by the place at first sight, and even Al stopped to take a few pictures with his phone.

While she waited for Bertha to climb down the steps of the bus, she chanced a glance at the man she was falling for. For the first time in her life, she had something to fight for beyond her own music career. Her life had new meaning, a new direction. But, could she follow that direction, or would she risk giving too much up?

A bigger question gnawed at her composure: was he enough for her to stay?

Michelangelo's dark hair had fallen in front of his eyes and he brushed it away. As if sensing her examination, he turned toward her. A smile stretched across his lips. He was in his element, and in his element he was truly happy.

Damn! Carly wanted him.

She hoped beyond measure this concert would succeed. Everything rested on it. Save the winery first and then she had a decision to make.

CHAPTER TWENTY-TWO

New Meaning

'Twenty euros is not enough!' Carly threw the ticket back into the basket Ms. Maxhammer held in her free hand. 'The maximum seating capacity of this vineyard is three hundred, and even if we sold out,' she calculated the math in her head. 'That would raise six thousand euros—not enough to save the winery.'

Ms. Maxhammer placed the basket by the entrance to the patio. She wore a spotless white pantsuit more suited to a fashion runway than a dilapidated vineyard. A chunky, golden chain necklace draped across her neck. 'Our other concerts were either free, or less than ten euros, so this is already a hefty price increase. You forget, we didn't come here to make a fortune. Maestro Braun raised the money himself to pay for the orchestra's expenses. This tour was a publicity stunt, no more.'

Carly's heart sunk. 'But Michelangelo needs the money now.'

'The trick is to get them here in the first place to see the beauty firsthand, then they'll spend their money. You worry about your aria, and I'll worry about the dollar signs.' Ms. Maxhammer winked at her and handed her a program. The president of the board had printed them this morning, with a picture of Michelangelo's winery on the front cover. The cover looked lovely, but it only served to remind Carly of what they had to lose.

'All right.' Carly sighed and walked to her seat in the orchestra. Ms. Maxhammer was a shrewd businesswoman. She could calculate funds better than a tax collector. Carly just had to trust her. She wasn't sure what Ms. Maxhammer had up her sleeve, but it had to be good.

The layout of the winery forced the crew to intersperse the audience amongst the rows of vines. It was hard to tell how many people were there. Spreading the audience out probably made it seem larger than it really was. Some chairs were empty.

Fighting her inner doubt, Carly plopped into her seat. The battle wasn't over yet. They still had a concert to play, and she owed Alaina a breathtaking aria.

Could she play her best?

She had to. Too much rested on this one performance. The concertmaster stood and signaled for her to give the first tuning note. The murmurs in the audience settled. Carly stuck her reed in her oboe with determination. She took a deep breath and played a soaring tuning note that resonated across the vineyard. The strings tuned, followed by the woodwinds and brass. Silence settled over the vineyard, punctuated by the chirps of finches.

Maestro Braun walked on stage in his penguin-tailed tux. Carly felt a rush of adrenaline as the audience applauded him and the orchestra tapped their feet in admiration. He acknowledged the audience then turned to the orchestra and raised his baton.

The first two pieces went well, giving Carly some confidence leading into the aria. The intermission came and Ms. Maxhammer walked on stage. Three members of Michelangelo's crew followed her, carrying bottles of wine, jewelry, and fine silk scarves. She announced an auction to the audience, and invited them to come up to the stage and bid.

Genius. But auctioning off pleasantries still wouldn't raise enough money to save the winery. If that's all Ms. Maxhammer had up her sleeve, they were doomed. Carly slipped into the office to change into her now-famous red dress for the aria.

Alaina stood at the mirror, fluffing her hair. She'd already changed into her glaring monstrosity and the sequins almost blinded Carly as she turned toward her.

Alaina caught her eye in her reflection. 'Quite a nice place. But I don't have to convince you now, do I?'

'What do you mean?'

'Come now, we both know you went for Michelangelo because of his winery.'

Carly's mouth dropped open. Panic rose up until she saw a smile creep into Alaina's mouth.

'I'm only joking.' Alaina clicked the cap back on her red lipstick. 'I hope you two are happy, even if you stole him.'

Carly shrugged, feeling as though she toyed with a prize she couldn't claim—a prize Alaina would die for. 'I haven't even figured out what I want. Congratulations are a little premature.'

'Well, if it's with him or someone else, I hope you do find love.' Alaina's tone had become surprisingly serious, making Carly glance up and meet her gaze.

The diva gave her a solemn nod, then went back to applying her mascara. Warmth spread through Carly. Maybe they had finally reached a good place together.

She hoped so, for her and the sake of the aria. 'I hope you find someone one of these days.' Carly pulled her dress over her head.

'Oh he's out there somewhere.' Alaina mused, looking out the window across the vineyards. 'But, for now, I have to focus on this aria. I have the famous, or should I say infamous, Christian Delacanto coming from the Gazzetta di Milan. He's come exclusively to critique our aria, per my request.'

Meaning, she'd paid him big bucks just to show up. Carly gulped, trying to convince herself they had a chance. 'Why did you choose him?'

'Because his opinion matters, and with our ratings so far, we need a gem of a quote to salvage anything at all from this entire tour.'

They had their work cut out for them, but Carly wasn't going to give up. She'd give Alaina the best accompaniment she could muster. For the first time, she thought Alaina deserved it.

'Let's give him something to talk about.' Carly zipped up the back of her dress and headed for the door.

A lot of the audience lingered on stage, gathering around the silent auction items. Ms. Maxhammer clapped her hands, signaling the end of intermission, and the concert-goers trickled off the stage back to their seats.

A surreal sense of displacement came over Carly, as though she was standing outside herself looking at a crucial moment in her own life. One blink and she saw herself running with Michelangelo's kids—her kids—down the rows of vines. The next blink, she was back in Boston, fighting the congestion to get to her gig on time.

A long note rang out, bringing her back to reality. The second oboe tuned the orchestra.

'Well, here goes nothing.' Alaina stood beside her, smoothing her dress down the front. Then, she reached over and touched Carly's arm gently. 'Two women singing about love—and neither of us can seem to get it right. What's that say about us, eh?'

For the first time, Alaina's wide eyes shone with vulnerability as she scanned the crowd.

Carly's confidence wasn't the only one shaken by the tour. For the first time, she felt bad for the diva. Not only did the woman think she'd stolen Michelangelo, but she'd also bombed on her big investment to push her career. She wasn't so different from Carly—sweating through the gigs, always looking for the next step up the ladder. If she had to pay to have her own solo, then she wasn't as established as she liked people to think. Carly's determination hardened. 'Let's show them we know what we're talking about.'

Maestro Braun invited them on stage, and the audience politely applauded as they walked in front of the orchestra. Scanning the audience, she saw Michelangelo sitting in the front row besides his mother, holding her hand. Signora Ricci smiled at Carly. The old woman narrowed her eyes and nodded reassuringly, as if she knew Carly could do it.

If that wasn't enough of a cue, then Carly didn't know what was. She brought her oboe to her lips, took a deep breath, and began the aria.

Only this time it didn't sound as though she was playing the same notes. Her music danced, freed of the constraints of the bar lines. Pure joy welled up within her, echoing the moment she had played with Michelangelo last night. That was love, and she finally could express it through her oboe. Bach had it right all along.

Alaina's eyebrow rose as she listened to the final bars of the prelude and took her breath to come in. Carly's joy was contagious, because Alaina's voice danced, light and buoyant on top of Carly's sound. Every beat fitted into place, and they swelled together in a lovely climax. The orchestra accompanied them in perfect harmony. Carly ended the solo, and her last note resonated over the vineyard, followed by the chirps of finches.

Applause erupted twice as loud as when they were introduced. The first row stood without Michelangelo's cue, and the second row, and the third. Alaina gestured to Carly, and they bowed together. The applause continued when they walked offstage, inviting them back for a second bow. The applause surged as Alaina came back on after Carly. The opera diva beamed as she waved to the crowd.

Carly looked for the critic and found him clapping wholeheartedly. Was that a smile that spread through his lips? But, she only truly cared about Michelangelo and his mother's reaction. They stood, smiling and clapping together, and she could almost picture them fifteen years younger, watching a concert together when his mother had taken care of him and not the opposite. She breathed with relief. *Mission accomplished.*

Ms. Maxhammer came onstage with two bouquets of wild flowers. 'Courtesy of Michelangelo. These are from his fields.'

Carly's throat tightened as Ms. Maxhammer handed her the first bouquet. *Maybe not the best idea in the world.* If Michelangelo had wanted to make amends with the soprano, he should have given her at least a few more days to cool off. Carly's heart sank as reality hit her. He didn't have a few days. They were getting on a plane tomorrow.

Alaina eyed the bouquet with skepticism. Would the diva make a scene and throw them on the stage?

'For me?' Alaina turned to Ms. Maxhammer.

'Yes, he specifically said to give you one, too.' Ms. Maxhammer gave her an encouraging nod. 'One of the reasons why he planned this concert was to make it up to you.'

Alaina gracefully accepted the bouquet with a poker face. She sniffed the flowers, then turned to Michelangelo in the audience.

Carly's fingers tightened over her bouquet, crushing the stems. *Here we go again.*

Alaina simply nodded, smiled at the audience, then walked off stage.

What? No temper tantrum, no finger-pointing? Carly followed her, baffled. As they walked back to their dressing room, Carly couldn't help but ask. 'You accepted his flowers?'

Alaina picked up the hem of her dress so the fabric wouldn't touch the grass. 'Why wouldn't I? Our aria was phenomenal. He gave us a chance to perform again, and we succeeded. You've already won him over. What else can I expect?'

'I just thought you'd…'

'Make a scene?' She waved her hand. 'I know when to throw in the towel—or in this case, the sour grapes. Besides, wouldn't want to leave a bad taste in Signore Delacanto's mouth after that beautiful performance now, would I?'

Carly almost choked with surprise. Even if Alaina had been gracious in order to impress the critic, her unexpected composure still impressed her. Maybe the diva could be reasonable after all.

Carly stopped in her tracks and turned toward her. 'I can't see why he'd have anything but praise. You really did sound like an angel.'

'That's because you played like one. Even if your dress was only half as beautiful as mine.'

Alaina gave Carly a half-smile that hinted she was only joking, and Carly laughed despite herself. 'I'll have to get an electric cord and a power source if I'm going to compete with that.'

Too bad the tour was over and they were no longer roommates. Carly was starting to like her.

CHAPTER TWENTY-THREE

Final Count

Michelangelo had squeezed his mother's hand as the final notes of the concert rang out. Even if they'd have to sell the vineyard, at least they'd have this night to remember. All of the commotion, the crowd and the music had awoken a part of his mother he hadn't seen in a long time. Even if she didn't understand exactly why they were there, she was at peace. The music distracted her, keeping the constant confusion of her degenerating disease at bay.

Not only was he enjoying himself with his mother, but Carly played as though she was on fire. She swayed to the music with her oboe, creating a synergy with Alaina that grew with every note they played together. It was impressive to watch and Michelangelo was proud of her.

If only he knew what went on in her heart.

He'd told himself he'd deal with the aftermath, but Carly's plane ride tomorrow already loomed over him, creeping in like a dark cloud whenever he let it. He couldn't make her stay. He'd never be able to live with himself if she gave up everything she'd built for herself back in Boston and was unhappy at the vineyard. He extended the invitation, and he showed her how he felt about her.

He'd done all he could do. Staying with him was a choice only she could make.

Besides, there might not *be* a vineyard when it came down to it. What was he thinking? He had nothing to offer her anyway. He and his mother might be homeless in the near future, and he should be planning to relocate. Michelangelo patted his mother's hand and swallowed his rising anxieties. They had this lovely moment and he wasn't about to waste it.

Maestro Braun thanked the audience and invited Ms. Maxhammer to the stage. The older woman shrugged off help and ascended the steps with her cane. She made her way to center stage and took the microphone.

'Let us first thank Maestro Braun and his talented orchestra for a truly lovely concert.'

The audience applauded as she shook the Maestro's hand.

'And next, Michelangelo Ricci, for allowing us to use this scenic place for our last performance.'

Michelangelo stood and Ms. Maxhammer gestured toward him. He wasn't sure she'd had time to tally the ticket sales, but from the size of the audience, it would only buy him a month or two at best.

As if reading his mind, Ms. Maxhammer added, 'May this gorgeous vineyard stand here for all time.'

She waited patiently as light applause welled up, then settled down. Michelangelo's heart rate increased. He should have had a bottle of his own wine.

'You—' she pointed to the audience as a spark lit her eyes. 'Have helped us with that task.'

Michelangelo sat on the edge of his seat. Was she going to announce how much they'd raised?

Ms. Maxhammer pulled a piece of paper from her pocket and unfolded it. 'According to initial reports, through ticket sales, the silent auction, and generous donations, we've managed to raise twenty thousand euros toward the preservation of this vineyard.'

Twenty thousand euros. Michelangelo tried to wrap his mind

around the large sum as the audience applauded. He was forever indebted to these Americans—the same people he'd once thought were lazy, selfish idiots. Their generosity humbled him. He couldn't have been more wrong about them. He didn't want their efforts to go in vain. Twenty thousand euros would certainly help. But would the offer be enough to beat Herb Ranger's?

Ms. Maxhammer pulled another piece of paper from her pocket. 'But we all know that won't be enough.'

Silence settled over the audience as she ripped open an envelope and pulled out what looked like a fancy check. 'So, I'd like to add another zero to that number.'

Two hundred thousand euros! Michelangelo's heart stopped. Struck by shock, he held onto both arms of his chair. He reclaimed some of his composure and raised his hand to get her attention. 'You don't have to do that.'

'I assure you I can, and I will.' Ms. Maxhammer answered him from the stage. Her shrewd business sense crept into her face as she narrowed her eyes. 'On the assumption this orchestra is welcome here each summer to play a concert.'

Michelangelo nodded slowly, then more empathetically. 'Of course they are.'

'Then, Mr. Ricci, come up to the stage and claim your check.'

He stood, incredulous. Was she really serious? Was his vineyard truly saved? Gazing down at his mother's happy face, he fought tears. She'd spend the rest of her years with some moments of peace and precious memories.

Mrs. Ricci pushed him toward the stage. 'Go on, you deserve it.'

Michelangelo stepped forward, feeling as though he was walking in a dream. Applause encouraged him all the way up to the stage. He gave Ms. Maxhammer a hug, whispering in her ear. 'I don't know how to repay you.'

She patted his back. 'You remind me of when I fell in love. You've brought this whole orchestra on a wonderful journey. Believe me, you already have.'

Carly wanted to break through the orchestra and celebrate with Michelangelo on stage. But too many obstacles stood in the way, and she wasn't even thinking about Bertha and the army of violins. The concert was over, the tour had ended, and Michelangelo had his winery. Now, she had to decide. If she got back on that plane, she'd have too many gigs waiting for her to stop and think about this again. If she didn't take the step now, she wouldn't do it all the way from Boston. Her obsessive musical life would give her no time to reflect, no time to look back.

What if she couldn't drum up the same gig balance she had in Boston? What if her relationship with Michelangelo fizzled out? She'd been a realist her whole life, and posing such questions only kept her true to herself.

Maybe that's the way it should be.

Her phone vibrated in her purse under her feet—another gig request or student already waiting for her response. The cord that tied her to her home was wound tightly, and she couldn't tell if it was a noose or a lifeline. Sometimes it felt like both.

'Aren't you happy for him?' Melody leaned over from the principal flautist's seat. 'He's done so much for us.'

'Of course I am.' Carly ran her cleaning cloth over her oboe.

'I thought you two had something going on there for a while.' Melody closed her music folder. It was the last time the Easthampton Civic Symphony would play that particular set.

Carly shrugged, feeling way too melancholy. 'All good things must come to an end.'

'Like this tour.' Melody gazed out over the vineyard and sighed. 'I'm going to miss Italy. Wolf and I made some great memories.' She turned back to Carly. 'But I'm sure you're eager to leave and get back to your gigs.'

Carly picked up her purse, afraid to check her phone. When the plane had landed in Italy all she had wanted to do was get to her messages and get back on another plane to Boston. Now she didn't know what she wanted.

'Carly?'

'Hmm?'

Melody's gaze bored into her as if her friend could see her soul. 'Is there something wrong?'

Carly glanced at the window of the room where she'd stayed with Michelangelo. The curtains wafted through the opening into the night breeze as if seeking her return. She tore her gaze away and turned back to her friend. 'I'm not sure.'

Melody scrunched her pretty nose. 'What do you mean you're not sure?'

Carly reached out and picked up Melody's hand. Her friend's engagement ring caught the light of the moon, shining like a star on her finger. Carly wondered if the rock ever weighed down Melody's hand. 'It's easy for you. You have nothing to lose.'

Melody nodded solemnly as if she knew now what this really was about. 'I should have told you more about my own struggles. At the time, I didn't think you'd understand.'

'Understand what?'

'Why I risked everything for Wolf.'

Risk? How could Melody ever know anything about risk? She had the best of both worlds. 'You didn't risk anything. You're both still in the orchestra, you have your gigs and he's here with you now.'

'Yes, it turned out very well for us both. But when we first got together, the board had a policy against him dating anyone in the orchestra. And if anyone found me with the conductor, they'd think I was trying to secure my own job by sleeping my way to the top. They would have kicked us both out.'

Carly shook her head. 'I had no idea you were going through so much.'

Melody patted the back of her hand. 'I'm sorry I didn't tell you. It would have brought you right into the mess along with us, and I didn't want your position questioned. I didn't want you

209

keeping secrets for me.'

Carly sighed, wondering when they'd stopped being so close. 'I would have.'

'I know you would. But that's not why I wanted to bring this up.' Melody gazed out into the audience. Carly could have sworn she was watching Michelangelo help his mother up from her seat. 'Sometimes love means taking risks.'

'Right.' Carly already knew that. The question was: was she willing to take the risk? Was she really in love? Melody couldn't answer that question for her. Carly had to figure it out herself.

Carly stood, ready to confront Michelangelo. It may be the last time she'd see him until the orchestra played there next year. She couldn't imagine coming back a year later and seeing again what she had passed up. Would Michelangelo have another girlfriend on his arm? 'Thanks for the advice.'

'Anytime.' Melody snapped her flute case shut and slipped her instrument into her bag. 'Guess I'll see you tomorrow on the plane?'

Carly's stomach tightened. Did she really want to go through with it and leave? It seemed as though the tide flowed against her will, and she could do nothing to stop it. 'Guess so.'

Now she had to tell Michelangelo.

Carly marched across the orchestra to where she'd last seen Michelangelo with his mother. The chairs were empty, so she followed the cobblestone path to the office. The door lay open. That had been her and Alaina's dressing room, so she didn't feel too weird going in. She heard voices from the corridor leading into the house. He was probably putting his mother to bed.

Should she leave without saying goodbye? Her carefully planned life waited for her back at home—her music group, her gigs, her orchestras, her friends. Would she lose her willpower if she saw him one last time? Carly's fingers brushed along an old shelf with pictures of Michelangelo's family on the vineyard. His father sat on a tractor wearing a straw hat and overalls, waving in the bright sun. Workers stood in front of a barrel twice their height with their arms around each others' shoulders. A young Michelangelo smiled while pretending to punch another boy with a broken nose and freckles. *Ricco.*

Carly picked up the picture and dusted off the glass. Ricco had left Michelangelo without a trace, and his disappearance without saying goodbye haunted him to this day. She couldn't do the same thing. She cared about him too much to hurt him in that way.

Just as Carly decided to wait, movement came from the corridor. The door opened and Michelangelo stepped in. His face brightened when he saw her.

'My dear Carls! What a marvelous performance.' He walked over and kissed the back of her hand fervently. 'Bravo!'

The mention of his new nickname for her burned her neck. 'Thank you. I think we finally got it right—and I have you to thank for that.'

'I merely provided the stage, nothing more.'

Carly blushed, wanting to tell him he provided much more than just a stage—the very essence of what it felt like to be in love—the one thing that damn aria needed. Instead, she pulled away. 'Congratulations. Your winery will be safe.'

'Thanks to you.' He pulled her close against him.

She allowed herself to relax in his embrace, letting the warmth and rush of adrenaline flow through her. The smell of his skin mixed with a trace of aftershave brought back memories of the previous night.

Michelangelo nuzzled his nose into her hair and sighed. 'Can you stay one more night?'

Carly shook her head. 'I'm afraid if I do I'll miss my plane.'

'So what?' He cupped her chin in his hand and forced her to look into his intense gaze. 'Stay here with me.'

Her heart pounded. This was what she was afraid of. Every ounce of her being pleaded with her logical mind. 'I can't.' Carly pulled away, and her chest ached as if she'd torn her heart, leaving a part of it with him. 'I can't make a lifetime's decision based on one night.'

He took her hand, smoothing his thumb over her skin. 'Come now, you've known me longer than one night.'

Carly rolled her eyes. 'Almost two weeks, then.'

Michelangelo kissed her fingers. 'Big difference.'

'No.' Carly took her hand back. 'You're tempting me.'

Michelangelo smiled, but it was sad. 'I had to try.'

'And I appreciate the offer.' Carly moved toward the door before she couldn't move any longer. 'I just need more time to think.'

'Plane rides are good for that.'

Yes, but what he didn't understand was when she got on that plane, it would already be too late. Carly forced herself to open the door. 'Thank you for everything.'

Michelangelo nodded. 'Don't forget about me, or Italy.'

Carly bit her lip and left without another word. If she returned to Boston that was exactly what she had to do.

CHAPTER TWENTY-FOUR

Take Off

Edda raised an eyebrow as Carly got on the orchestra bus. 'Wasn't expecting you.' Her thick Italian accent only reminded Carly of Michelangelo.

'Just forgot something.' Carly smiled and passed by her as if nothing had happened. She didn't need an Italian mother to guilt-trip her into thinking about what she was giving up. She knew what she was doing.

She was the last one on, and the only seat left was, of course, next to Al. Already cursing her decision, she made her way down the aisle and plopped down next to the trombonist.

Al adjusted his Red Sox cap. 'About time you showed up. You know I had to ride alone all the way up here?'

That's right. She'd driven up with Michelangelo to 'get ready' for the concert. When, in fact, they'd spent the night catching up on lost time.

Carly pushed the fresh slew of delicious memories away. She was a classical oboist, not a wine-brewer. 'Well, I'm here now.'

Al leaned back in his seat and gave her an appraising look as if wondering what went wrong with her Italian boyfriend. 'So you are.'

He pulled out his phone. 'I'll even let you play the first round.'

Carly was not in the mood for empty distractions. *Angry Birds* wasn't going to solve anything. 'You go ahead.' As the ache in her chest grew to a full-fledged throbbing, she laid her head back against the seat and closed her eyes.

Worse news greeted her at the hotel. Her room was empty, dark, and cold and smelled like a moldy air conditioner. Alaina had decided to take her own private jet that night, leaving Carly alone the one night she would have enjoyed company.

At least she had her phone. What she should do was go through her messages and prepare her schedule so when she got back to Boston she had gigs and students lined up.

Carly threw her oboe case on the bed. Not an ideal bed companion. She could be sleeping beside Michelangelo.

Stop dreaming and get to work.

She clicked on the screen and accessed her e-mail account. Fifty-eight e-mails awaited her reply. Methodically, she did what she did best, organizing them according to importance, then answering each one with the only answer she knew how to give. Yes.

Yes, she'd drive three hours to Maine to play at some small wedding ceremony on a Saturday afternoon. Yes, she'd accept a new oboe student at her home studio. It only meant getting up a half hour earlier on a Sunday. What did it matter to her? She had no one to stay up late with, especially with Melody on the track to marriage.

All of a sudden each e-mail became an empty pursuit. The scheduling process didn't bring her the same joy she once had, the joy she now had with Michelangelo. The joy she'd just thrown away like a piece of trash.

Anger and frustration brimmed inside her. She'd become a slave to her work. Why the hell couldn't she just let go?

Carly threw her phone across the room. It bounced off the wall and landed under the bed. Tears stung her eyes and she viciously wiped them away. The truth was she was scared. Scared of a life that wasn't all music; a life with variables she couldn't control. But could she live her life tied to her oboe? Or did she want something more?

After graduating from New England Conservatory, Carly had taken every opportunity she had, until scheduling each gig became a robotic pursuit, trying to fit as many jobs in one weekend and as many students in each day as possible. It took over her life before she could even start one.

But she didn't care then. So why did she care now?

The truth hit her like a wrecking ball, cracking through her carefully constructed ideal of who she thought she was and what she thought she wanted to accomplish. Music wasn't how many gigs you had, how many concertos you memorized, or how many orchestras you played with. It's who you played them with, who you played them for. Not a faceless bunch of critics, but for the people who mattered in your life. She'd found the true meaning to music at Michelangelo's side.

*****

The sun beat down hot and strong, reminding Michelangelo of the days when he and Ricco would sneak away to the stream that ran alongside his father's lands. They'd strip down to their boxers and wade in the cool water, splashing each other until they shivered with goose bumps.

Michelangelo wiped the sweat from his brow as he dug holes for the scaffolding into the newly cleared ground. The smell of wet earth and wildflowers wafted up. Usually it calmed him. 'Put the new trellises over there.'

'Si, Signore.' Rodolfo nodded and helped the crew move the beautiful weave work that would stabilize another crop's growth. Behind them, finches chirped and insects buzzed in the usual symphony that accompanied his vineyard.

One day after the concert, orders were already coming in for whole crates of wine. The press from the concert alone sky-rocketed his winery from obscure isolation into coveted popularity. People were asking about booking tours and tastings, and Isabella was already demanding another office secretary to handle the incoming e-mails and calls.

A young boy walked across the fields. At first, he thought Isabella's son had grown overnight, but then he recognized the slicked-back oily hair and the dark, pensive eyes.

Michelangelo dropped his shovel and met the boy halfway, his arms crossed over his chest. 'Look who's turned up.'

'I want a job.' The boy kicked at a sod of dirt as he spoke, but at the end he looked him straight in the eye. He'd changed his clothes, wearing cleaner jeans and a collared shirt he must have got from some second-hand store. At least he'd had the good sense to show up clean—even if he hadn't combed his hair.

'Is that so?' Michelangelo gestured toward the house. 'Have you talked to Isabella?'

'Yes…sir.' The boy added the second word as if he wasn't used to addressing authority. 'She said to talk to you.'

Michelangelo picked up a shovel off the ground and handed it to him. 'We can always use workers like you. What's your name?'

'Paolo.'

'Paolo.' He half expected him to say Ricco. But he refused to be disappointed. Even if he didn't find Ricco, he could take in a dozen boys like him from the streets. It wouldn't change what his father had done, but it might stop it from happening again. 'Come on, Rodolfo will get you started with everything you need to know.'

He led the boy to the new patch of soil where they were setting up the trellises. Everything was going better than he'd ever dreamed. So why did his heart sink in his chest like a wet sod?

He checked his watch. Eleven twenty-three. Carly's plane would have taken off a half hour ago. He knew because he'd booked the flight for them when he planned the tour.

Give it up. A concert oboist wouldn't like getting her hands dirty with pruning, or her feet stained by crushing grapes. Who was he kidding? She was better off in Boston, and he had a winery to maintain. A thriving one at that. He owed it to Ms. Maxhammer to make sure her efforts weren't in vain.

Movement caught his eye from the patio up the hill. Was Isabella coming out to make sure Paolo showed up and did the work? She could be a formidable woman if you crossed her.

Blonde hair caught the rays of sun. Michelangelo dropped his shovel. That wasn't Isabella.

Carly ran to the edge of the patio and raised her hand to her brow to shield her eyes from the sun. She gazed down at the hillside where he worked. Too stunned to move, Michelangelo watched as she ran down the hill toward him.

'You'd better go see to the signorina.' Rodolfo nudged him in the shoulder. 'Wouldn't want her falling down and breaking one of her fingers.'

Disbelief crashed through him. How was she here? Did the plane have a delay? Michelangelo moved slowly at first, then picked up speed. Surely Ms. Maxhammer would have contacted him had any change to the schedule been made. Carly was here for one reason alone. His heart sped with all the enormous possibilities. She'd chosen to stay.

Carly reached him just as he skidded down the hill. She rushed into his arms and he picked her up, never again wanting to let go.

'I thought you had a plane to catch.' He nuzzled his nose into her hair, breathing in her scent and the feel of her smooth skin as her cheek rubbed against his.

'I couldn't do it. I couldn't leave.' Carly tightened her grip, smoothing her hands along his back. Her touch made his nerves burst into flame.

He pulled his head back to meet her eyes. 'Why?'

She swallowed deeply as if gaining courage. Her fingertip traced his cheek. 'I was afraid to leave my musical life. I was afraid love

218

would distract me and ruin everything I've worked for.'

He listened, breathless. 'And did it?'

Carly smiled. 'I realized everything I worked for has led me to love, it's led me to you.' Joy like he'd never felt before erupted in his chest. He laughed deliriously, holding her against him.

Carly pulled away, crossing her arms. 'What's so funny?'

Michelangelo put his hands on her shoulders, realizing the truth as he said it. 'I love you, too.'

THE END